"We all need someone at some point."

Gavin's mouth was so beautifully sculpted, and Nike was grateful that he couldn't read her mind. He couldn't know how much he'd distracted her, especially at night when she tried to fall asleep. She kept thinking what it would be like to have him hold her, kiss her....

"I can't need any man who is in the military, Gavin. Never again."

Gavin smiled down at her and watched her lips part. "It's a good first step, don't you think?"

Seeing that gleam come to his eyes, Nike ached even more for his touch. The tension swirled between them.

"There are no other steps," she warned him.

"I don't believe that," Gavin said, his voice a low growl. Reaching out, he took that step forward. He leaned down, searching, finding her sweet mouth.

The world exploded within her. Her arms swept across his shoulders as his mouth captured hers, asking her to give in and participate fully.

Dear Reader,

I'm thrilled to be writing once again about the famous all-female Apache combat helicopter squadron known as the **BLACK JAGUAR SQUADRON**! I have received so much mail over the years that when given a chance to create a second squadron, BJS 60, I jumped at it.

I hope you enjoy *His Woman in Command*. This is the first of three books featuring the daring women pilots of this all-female combat squadron.

I have friends who have lived in Afghanistan and personally met some Afghani at the Tucson gem show over the years. The people are exceptional and I look forward to acquainting you with them, their customs, their integrity and courage. In this first book, we meet Captain Nike Alexander. She is an assertive, kick-butt, taking-names kind of woman. When she meets macho U.S. Army Captain Gavin Jackson, who heads up an A-team, things heat up in a hurry. Follow her life and times in Afghanistan. She's in command!

As always, I love to hear from my readers. Just e-mail me at muted29081@mypacks.net. Keep up with my busy writing schedule on my Web site, www.lindsaymckenna.com. Or catch me at www.eHarlequin.com with a blog or two.

Warmly,

Lindsay McKenna

LINDSAY McKENNA

His Woman in Command

Silhouette®
Romantic
SUSPENSE

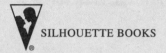 SILHOUETTE BOOKS

Recycling programs
for this product may
not exist in your area.

ISBN-13: 978-0-373-27669-1

HIS WOMAN IN COMMAND

Printed in U.S.A.

Books by Lindsay McKenna

LINDSAY MCKENNA

As a writer, Lindsay McKenna feels that telling a story is a way to share how she sees the world she lives in. Love is the greatest healer of all and the books she creates are parables that underline this belief. Working with flower essences, another gentle healer, she devotes part of her life to the world of nature to help ease people's suffering. She knows that the right words can heal and that a story can be a catalyst in a person's life. And in some way she hopes that her books may educate and lift the reader in a positive manner. She can be reached at www.lindsaymckenna.com.

To ROMVETS, a group of women who have served or are currently serving in the military. This list comprises women who are aspiring writers and published authors. It's an honor to be among you.
www.romvets.com.

Chapter 1

"Twenty bucks says you can't get that good-lookin' woman to come over to our table and have a beer with us," Staff Sargeant Neal Robles challenged.

Captain Gavin Jackson, leader of a ten-man Special Forces team, squinted in the semidarkness of the officers' club—a tent on the most dangerous border in the world: between Afghanistan and Pakistan. It was the last day of their two weeks of rest between month-long assignments in the field. Tomorrow, they'd be back out in the badlands border area hunting Taliban. Gavin sat with his nine men. The pitcher of frothy cold beer in front of them went quickly.

The woman in question had just entered the spacious tent, catching the attention of every man in the room. She was about five foot eight, with short, curly black hair framing an oval face and high cheekbones. She was olive-skinned with light gold eyes. Then there was her killer mouth that

Gavin wanted to capture and kiss. The frumpy green one-piece flight uniform that told him she was a pilot couldn't hide her assets. Curvy in all the right places. Gavin felt his body harden with desire.

He didn't know why. His relationship with another woman army pilot had crashed and burned a year ago. Gavin had sworn off women for now and women army pilots forever. Squirming in his seat, the wooden chair creaking, he shrugged as Neal Robles grinned like a wolf over the dare.

"Why her?" Gavin grunted, lifting the cold mug of beer to his lips.

Robles's dark brown eyes gleamed as he whispered, "She's hot, Cap'n."

"She's the *only* female in here," Gavin drawled. Indeed, the huge dark green canvas tent was packed with men— A teams coming in for a well-deserved rest, logistics, pilots or mechanics to support their missions. Women pilots were few, but they did exist. Automatically, Gavin rubbed his chest in memory of Laurie Braverman, the U.S. Army CH-47 Chinook driver that he'd fallen in love with. They'd broken up because of their mutual inability to compromise. A war of egos had eventually destroyed their relationship.

"She might be the only one," Robles asserted, "but you gotta admit, Cap'n, she's something." Robles looked at the other enlisted men around the table, all of whom bobbed in unison to agree with his observation.

Tugging on his recently trimmed beard, Gavin gave them an amused look. His team knew about his hard luck with Laurie, especially since he'd been a growly old bear for a month after their spectacular parting. "You know," he said, "it's damned hard enough to survive the border villages. Now, you want to collectively throw me at *another* driver?"

Driver was a common slang expression for any pilot whether they flew fixed-wing aircraft or helicopters.

Laughter rippled through his team. Gavin was fiercely protective of his men. They'd been together over here nearly a year, and they were tighter than a set of fleas on a mangy Afghan dog. He wanted to bring all of them back off this tour alive so they could go home to their families. He had visited the base barber this morning, got a wonderful hot shower, a trim, clean clothes and joined his men at the canteen tent. Although they were in the U.S. Army, their clothes were decidedly Afghani. With their beards, wearing their wool *pakols,* or caps, they melted into the mountainous area less a target as a result of their wardrobe. They all wore the traditional turban. The loose, comfortable-fitting top with long sleeves had pajamalike trousers of the same color, and the traditional wool vests were worn over it.

"Naw, she doesn't look like she's a man-eater like the last one you tangled with," Robles said. The table broke out in collective laughter once again. More beer was poured. A bartender came over and delivered another pitcher of cold beer, the froth foaming up and over of the top.

Gavin couldn't disagree and his gaze wandered to the woman leaning up against the makeshift bar and ordering a cup of coffee, not beer. She was probably on duty, Gavin assumed. He watched her hands. They were long, narrow and beautiful-looking. No wedding ring. But then, what did that mean? Nothing, because military combatants were forbidden to wear jewelry of any kind. So, she could be married. Frowning, Gavin felt his assistant CO, Dave Hansen, give his right shoulder a nudge.

"Go on, Gavin," he said in his slow Texas drawl, "she looks pretty docile. Invite her over. We'd all like the company of a good-lookin' woman to remind us of what's waiting for us at home. We're harmless. Just tell her we're voyeurs."

Gavin scowled at his team. "Since when are you willing to throw me to the lions? Don't I treat you right out there?"

Guffaws broke out and Gavin couldn't help grinning. They all desperately needed a little fun. The border country was violent and lethal. They'd spent thirty days in the mountains hunting out pockets of Taliban in caves. Not that the local villages along the border ever cooperated. Most of them were terrorized by the Taliban. And the tribal people had been forgotten by the government in Kabul decades ago. Out there, Gavin knew, no fiercely independent Afghan could be trusted once your back was turned on them. They'd just as soon put a bullet between your shoulder blades as look at you because of what the Taliban had done to them. Gavin's team had had several firefights with the Taliban on their last mission. If not for the Apache helo drivers coming in with heavy fire support, they wouldn't be here enjoying this beer with one another.

Gavin sat up and sighed. He knew his men needed a reprieve from their deadly work. They all had PTSD symptoms. Why not waltz up to this gal and ask her to join them? "Okay," he growled at them, "I'll go throw myself on her mercy for the likes of all of you and see what she says."

The men clapped and cheered as Gavin stood up. He smoothed down his vest and adjusted the thick leather belt around his waist that carried a dagger and a pistol. Out in the field, he'd have body armor on, but not now. He adjusted the dark brown wool *pakol* on his head. To anyone seeing these men riding up on their tough mountain-bred ponies, they looked like a group of Afghan men. Of course, here in the canteen tent, they were out of place, but everyone on base knew Special Forces A teams dressed like Afghans.

Giving his group a wink, Gavin said, "Okay, men, keep it down while I work some magic." They all nodded solemnly, lifted their glasses of beer and beamed excitedly like little children waiting for Christmas to arrive. Gavin shook his head and walked across the creaking plywood floor toward the bar. He noticed that although men were hanging around the bar, all of them gave the woman pilot some room to breathe. Not that they weren't looking at her. But none made a move on her. Why? They were support and logistics men and worked in the camp, so they might know something about this woman pilot he didn't.

Coming to the bar, Gavin stood about two feet away from her. The scalding look she gave him with those lion-gold eyes surprised him. He was clean, for once. He didn't smell of sweat and fear. His black hair and beard were neatly trimmed and combed. Maybe she didn't like A teams or Afghans, Gavin decided. The way her full mouth thinned, her hands tense around the white ceramic mug of coffee, told him everything. She really didn't want this intrusion into her space.

"I'm Captain Gavin Jackson," he said, pushing aside his fear of rejection. He looked at the upper arm of her green flight suit. "We've never seen a patch with a black cat on it. I was wondering what squadron you're with." That was a safe icebreaker, Gavin thought.

Nike Alexander, at twenty-six, did not want any male attention. Just a year ago, she'd lost Antonio, an officer in the Peruvian Army who had died in a vicious firefight with cocaine dealers. She glared icily at the man, who was decidedly handsome despite his rugged appearance. "I'm with the Black Jaguar Squadron 60," she snapped.

"I've been out here on the front nearly a year. I've never seen this patch. Is this a new squadron?" Gavin opted for something simpler than trying to get this good-looking woman to come over to their table for a beer. He was frantically searching for ways to defuse her tension.

Shrugging, Nike lifted the coffee to her lips, took a sip and then said, "We're basically Apache pilots in an all-woman flight program. We got here three weeks ago."

"Oh." Gavin didn't know what to think about that. "All women?"

Nike's mouth twitched. "We're black ops." His thick, straight brows raised with surprise. While it was true there were women pilots in combat, no women-only squadrons existed. "We're top secret to the rest of the world. Here at camp, they know what we do," she added to ward off questions she saw in his large blue eyes.

Under other circumstances, Nike would be interested in this warrior. Clearly, he was an A-team leader. She knew these brave and hardy Special Forces teams were on the front lines, finding Taliban and stopping their incursion into Afghanistan's space. His hands were large, square and roughened by work and the forces of the weather.

"Ah, black ops," Gavin murmured. He saw the wariness in her gold eyes. "You're new?"

"I arrived a week ago."

"Welcome aboard," he said, holding out his hand toward her. This time, he was sincere. Anyone who flew the border risked their lives every time they lifted off from this secret base.

Looking at his proffered hand and then up at him, Nike couldn't help herself and slid her hand into his. He grinned like a little boy given a Christmas gift. Despite the neatly trimmed beard that gave his square face a dangerous look, he seemed happy to meet her. Well, they were both in the army and that meant something. Her flesh tingled as his fingers wrapped gently around hers. She admired his deeply sunburned face, laugh lines at the corners of his eyes. A wild, unexpected surge of excitement coursed through Nike. What was *that* all about? Why was her heart pounding? She broke the contact and pulled her hand away.

Oh, he was eye candy, there was no doubt. The boyish, crooked grin made him even more devastatingly handsome, Nike decided.

"What's your name?" Gavin asked. He forced his hands off the bar, unexpectedly touching her olive-tone skin. The brief contact sent crazy tingles up and down his arm. The close proximity to this woman intoxicated him in quite another way. Gavin fully realized he was more than a little tipsy from the beer he and his team had been guzzling. But he was still alert, still fixated on this new person of interest.

"I'm Captain Nike Alexander," she informed him in a clipped and wary tone. She'd just arrived with her squadron from the USA and wanted to focus only on the mission before them. As an all-woman squadron they had a lot to prove—again. They'd done it in Peru, now it would be here. She didn't want to tangle with some sex-hungry A-team leader who hadn't seen a woman in God knew how long. Still, a secret part of her wondered what Gavin would look like without that beard. Not that he wasn't handsome with it; maybe she was just more interested than she cared to admit.

"Nike," he murmured, rolling the name around on his tongue. "That's different." He squinted and gave her a measuring look. "Are you…American?" Her husky voice had a trace of an accent. When she frowned, he knew he'd asked the wrong question.

"I was born in Athens, Greece, Captain. I was invited from my country to train and work for the U.S. Army." She turned and showed the American flag on the left shoulder of her uniform.

"Greek." That made sense, although he'd said it as if he were stunned by the information. Seeing the frustration in her large, clear gold eyes, Gavin asked, "Wasn't Nike a goddess in Greek myths?"

"She still is," Nike said in a flat tone. "I was named after her."

"I see." Gavin stood there, his brows dipping. "So, you're part of a black ops, you're a female pilot and you're from Greece." Brightening, he shared a look with her, his smile crooked. "That makes you a pretty rare specimen out here in our back country."

"You're making me feel like a bug under a microscope, Captain. Why don't you mosey back to your team. I'm not interested in anything but my mission here."

Her tone was low and dismissive.

Gavin kept his smile friendly and tried to appear neutral and not the leering, sexually hungry male he really was. It was now or never. "Speaking of that, Captain Alexander, we were wondering if you might not come and join us? My boys and I are going back for thirty more days in the bush tomorrow morning. We'd enjoy your company."

Easing into a standing position, Nike glanced over at the table. Nine other bearded men in Afghan dress looked hopefully in her direction. English-speaking women who were not Moslem were a rarity in this country. Of course they'd want her company. "Captain, I'm not the USO.

And I'm not for sale at any price. If you want female entertainment I suggest you find it somewhere else."

Ouch. Gavin scowled. "Just a beer, Captain. Or, we'll buy you another cup of coffee. That's all. Nothing else." He held up both his hands. "Honest."

"I appreciate the offer," Nike said. She pulled out a few coins from her pocket and put them on the bar next to the drained cup of coffee. "But I must respectfully decline, Captain." She turned and marched out of the tent.

"That went well," Gavin said, his grin wide and silly-looking as she exited. He walked over to his men, who looked defeated.

"You crashed and burned," Robles groaned.

Jackson poured himself another glass of beer. "She's got other fish to fry." He said it as lightly as he could.

The men nodded and nursed their beers.

At twenty-eight, Gavin understood that a little fun and laughter was good medicine for his men. Silently, he thanked Nike Alexander for her decision. What would it have been like to have her come over and sit with them? It would have lifted their collective spirits. They were starving for some feminine attention. Oh, she probably realized this, but didn't get that his invitation was truly harmless. Gavin had seen a lot of sensitivity in her face and read it in her eyes. However, she was protective, if not a little defensive about sharing that side. He couldn't blame her.

Gavin told them what he'd found out. His men were like slavering dogs getting a morsel tossed to them. In Afghanistan, Moslem women could not talk directly to any man. Consequently, it was a world of males with males and the women were hidden away in their homes. Gavin missed being stateside. Even though he'd crashed and burned with

Laurie Braverman on his first tour here, he still hungered for conversation with an intelligent woman.

As he glanced toward the flap of the tent where Nike Alexander had marched through, Gavin lamented her departure. Clearly, she thought he was hitting on her. Well, wasn't he? Digging into the pocket of his trousers, he produced a twenty-dollar bill and threw it across the table to his medic. "Here, Robles. Satisfied?"

Chuckling, Neal took the twenty and hoisted it upward. "You tried. Hey, Cap'n, this will give us another round of beer!"

The men clapped and hooted, and Gavin grinned crookedly. His team needed this kind of blowout before they got dropped in the badlands again. As he took one more look to where Nike had left, he wished he'd had a little more time with her. Would they ever meet again? Hope sprang in his chest. Nike was a fascinating woman, pilot or not. Gavin shrugged off any romantic thoughts and took a deep swig of beer. Chances of *ever* seeing Nike Alexander again were next to nothing.

"Nike," Major Dallas Klein-Murdoch said, "sit down and relax. Welcome to BJS 60."

Nike settled in front of her commanding officer's desk. Every incoming pilot to the squadron did a one-on-one with the CO. This morning, it was her turn. Dallas Klein's reputation with the original Black Jaguar Squadron, for which she had flown in Peru, was legendary. Nike was only too thrilled to be here under this woman's command. They'd had a stint together in Texas chasing Mexican drug-runners before this latest assignment. There, Dallas had fallen in love with ATF agent Mike Murdoch. The Pentagon had then sent Dallas and her new husband to Afghanistan to oversee the latest Black Jaguar Squadron. Murdoch was now a captain in the U.S. Army and worked as a strategy and operations officer for the all-women Apache combat pilots that comprised BJS 60. And while the pilots were all female, some males in the ranks took care of the Apache helicopters. Nike was glad that Dallas was assigned here with her new husband. Taking off her baseball cap, Nike sat down and grinned. "Like old times, isn't it?"

Dallas laughed. "Better believe it." She reached for a file folder and handed it to Nike. "Here are your orders. We have twenty women Apache pilots here and ten helicopters assigned to us. The last two helos are being flown in today to this base. My executive officer, XO, is going to be Captain Emma Trayhern-Cantrell."

Raising her brows, Nike said, "From *the* Trayhern family?"

"The very same. Shortly after you left Peru, Emma was assigned to BJS in Peru and flew Apaches down there for six months before I was able to convince the Pentagon to have her assigned here. She's a chip off the old Trayhern block—a real woman warrior."

"Whose child is she?" Nike wondered.

"Clay and Alyssa Cantrell-Trayhern's oldest child. Emma has three younger sisters, two of whom are in the U.S. Naval Academy right now. They're due to graduate next year. They're twins. Clay and Alyssa were Navy pilots and flew P3 antisubmarine aircraft for twenty years. Emma, whom you'll meet sometime today, is a long, lean red-haired greyhound with blazing gray eyes. I'm glad to have her on board. She's a natural XO."

Chuckling, Nike opened the folder. "Emma sounds perfect for this black ops."

"Oh, she is. Her grandfather is the original black-ops

figure behind the scenes," Dallas drawled, smiling. "Let's get down to business. I'm seeing my pilots individually to give them their orders."

"Fire away," Nike murmured, studying the papers.

"First of all, BJS 60 remains an all-woman U.S. Army force," Dallas began, leaning back in her chair. "The women I chose for this new squadron have more than one flight skill. For example, you are licensed to fly fixed-wing, single-engine planes as you did on the U.S.-Mexico border with me. And you're also certified to fly the CH-47, which is the workhorse helicopter used here in Afghanistan." Dallas looked over at the lean, wiry pilot. "Every woman in BJS 60 has multiskills in aviation. There may be times when I want you to fly the CH-47 and not the Apache."

"Being multitalented has never been a problem for me," Nike said, grinning.

Dallas leaned back in her chair. "We are under General Chapman and we work indirectly with the national Afghanistan Army. BJS 60 is going to be a 'sparrowhawk' team that will be called upon in emergencies when the regular Apache pilots from the other two squadrons are not available. In other words, we're going to pick up the slack to ensure that Special Forces A teams get immediate help and support out in the field. Our jobs will vary depending upon what General Chapman's operations officer decides for us. One day you could be flying a CH-47, another, you'll be back in the seat of an Apache helicopter. Mike, my husband, is working as a liaison between Chapman's people and us. We're going to try and get as much air time as possible in the Apache, but we also know our pilots will be flying other helicopters, too."

Nike nodded. Instantly, she pictured Captain Gavin Jackson, who was a man's man, supremely confident. Someone she was drawn to, but Nike wasn't willing to admit that to herself now or ever. "I ran into one of the A teams over at the canteen a little while ago."

"Yes, they're our front-line defense here on the border," Dallas told her. "These men go out for thirty days at a time. They are hunting Taliban and stopping terrorist insurgence from getting into Afghanistan. This is one of the most dangerous places in the world for our troops—the mountains and the border around the Khyber Pass, which connects Pakistan and Afghanistan."

"And we thought Peru was dangerous," Nike joked, turning the page in the file for her assignment.

"Yeah," Dallas said grimly. "This is worse. Let's talk about your assignment tomorrow morning. Part of a new project that's being initiated by the top generals now assigned to Afghanistan is winning the hearts and minds of the border villages in this country. Tomorrow BJS 60 pilots will be assigned to certain A teams to fly them into Taliban-controlled villages. The dudes in Washington, D.C., have finally figured out that if we don't make these boundary villages pro-American, we've lost the battle to stop terrorists from coming into this country from Pakistan."

"Why are these villages pro-Taliban?" Nike wondered, perplexed.

"They aren't. First of all, Afghanistan is composed of fiercely independent tribal systems. Even the Russians, who threw ten times the troops into this country, couldn't defeat the Mujahideen. Afghans don't count on anyone to help them. They have survived thousands of years with their tribal clans. In this century, the Afghan government, which has tried to force these different tribes or clans to acknowledge them, has failed to solidify them. The central government has always ignored the mountain villages along the border, anyway. They never poured any money, medical help, education or food from the government into these villages. Basically, the Kabul government didn't think ignoring these border villages was a problem until Osama bin Laden surfaced. Now, it's our biggest problem thanks to the government's blind eye."

Tightening her lips, Dallas added, "Kabul has Afghans who defy their own central government. They remain faithful only to their tribe and their chieftain or sheik. The Taliban uses force against the villagers, attacks their women and creates hostility among the tribal people. That is why these border villages don't stop Taliban and terrorists from coming and going through their valleys. They hate them as much as we do, but they lack the resources to stop the Taliban from being the bullies on the block. And Kabul officials never sent out troops to protect these border villages from the raiding Taliban, so the villagers are understandably distrustful of the central government. And your demeanor toward these villagers will be as follows. If you, as a person, do something good for an Afghan, they will call you *brother* or *sister* until they die. They are completely loyal to those who treat them humanely and with respect. That is what I want you to cultivate as you interface with the villagers. This is the only way we are going to win their hearts and minds."

"Nice to see these outlying villages hate the Taliban as much as we do. I'll be happy to 'make nice' with these village folks," Nike said.

"This new program the general has just initiated is beginning to bear fruit. Starting tomorrow, you're going to fly an A team to Zor Barawul, a village that is located five miles away from the Pakistan border. This A team will stay thirty days to try and win the trust and respect of these villagers. This operation, which is along all of the border, is to get villagers to realize that Americans are here to help them. We're not coming in like the Taliban with guns blazing and using brute force upon them. Furthermore, the medic in each of these A teams will be bringing in all kinds of medicine for villagers. We want to gain their trust with positive and consistent care. The only medical help these people have had in the last sixty years has been from Christian church missions and Sufi medical doctors who try their best to go from village to village helping the people."

"Sufis? I thought they were Moslem."

"Yes, they are. Sufis are the mystical branch of the Moslem religion. They are about peace, not war. Love and compassion instead of hatred and prejudice. We need more of that here and the Sufis are leading the way."

Nike raised her brows. "Then Sufis are the antithesis of the Moslem terrorists, aren't they?"

Dallas nodded. "Yes, and the Taliban is willing to kill the Sufi doctors who give their life to serving the village people, if they can. The terrorists are one end of the Moslem religion, Nike. They don't represent the middle or the other end, which is the Sufi sect. Now, General Chapman wants to expand upon that humanitarian mission and bring in A teams to support what they're doing."

"Isn't that dangerous—to put an A team down in a Taliban-controlled village?"

"Yes, it is," Dallas said. "But the new general, who is taking over the country insofar as military help for the Afghans, sees that this is the only way to change the border."

Nike was disappointed that she wouldn't be flying the

Apache right off the bat. She kept that to herself. "I wouldn't want to be an A team, then," Nike muttered.

"Fortunately, all you have to do is fly the CH-47 transport helicopter and drop them and their supplies off to the village and fly back here. I'm assigning you to six A teams that will be dropped along the border. When they need anything, you'll be at their beck and call via radio. If they request more medicine, you'll get the supplies from our base here and fly it in to them. If they need food, blankets or clothing, same thing. If they need ammo or weapon resupply, you'll be on call to support that, too."

"Sounds pretty routine," Nike said, hoping to have an Apache strapped to her butt so she could give the troops air support.

Shrugging, Dallas said, "Don't be so sure. The possibility of a Taliban soldier disguised as a villager sending a rocket up to knock your helo out of the sky is very real."

"Except for a tail gunner, I won't have any other weapons at my disposal to ensure that doesn't happen," Nike griped, unhappy. Each CH-47 had an enlisted tail gunner who doubled as the load master for the helicopter.

"We'll be flying Apache support for you," Dallas promised. "We're not going to leave you out there without proper air protection." She saw the unhappy look in Nike's eyes and understood her resignation. Nike was a combat warrior, one of the finest. But not all her BJS 60 pilots were accredited to fly the CH-47 as she was. "Look, don't go glum about this assignment. See what unfolds. Your work, as mundane as it might seem, is high-risk and important."

"I think I'll strap on a second .45. You can call me two-gun Alexander."

Dallas grinned at the Greek woman's response. Picking up another file, she said, "The border area is the Wild West and Dodge City, Nike. For real. It doesn't get any more dangerous than here. Here's your first assignment—the A team you're flying out at 0530. Once you drop them off, you fly back here and we'll give you the next village flight assignment."

Opening the order, Nike gasped. "Oh my God."

"What?"

Nike looked up, a pained expression crossing her face. "I just had a run-in with this dude, Captain Gavin Jackson, over at the canteen."

Smiling slightly, Dallas said, "I hope it went well."

"Not exactly."

Chapter 2

Their air commander was Captain Nike Alexander. Gavin couldn't believe his eyes that morning as his team trooped across the tarmac to the waiting CH-47 that would take them to the Taliban-controlled village of Zor Barawul.

He didn't know whether to give her an evil grin of triumph or simply keep a poker face. As he approached the opened rear of the CH-47s ramp, she was coming out of the right-hand seat, helmet dangling in her hand. When their eyes met, she instantly scowled.

Ouch. Gavin threw his pack behind the seat and pushed the rest of his gear beneath the nylon webbing. Looking up, he noticed her pursed lips and her narrowed golden eyes—on him.

"Don't worry," he told her teasingly, "I'm not infectious."

Nike couldn't help but grin. Despite Jackson's ragged Afghan clothing and that beard, he was undeniably handsome. A part of her wanted him. The merriment dancing in his dark blue eyes made her heart race just a little. "Don't worry, I'm vaccinated against guys like you." He merely smiled at her obvious warning. Damn, why did he have to be so good-looking?

Nike threaded between the other nine men who were settling in on either side of the cargo hold. She strolled down the ramp toward her load master, Andy Peters. The sergeant stood at the bottom waiting for everyone to get settled before he started loading the many boxes. Her boots thunked hollowly against the corrugated aluminum surface. On one side rested a fifty-caliber machine gun that Peters would put into a hole at the center of the ramp. Once airborne, Andy would drop the ramp, the ugly muzzle of the machine gun pointed down at the earth below them. Peters's job was to take out any Taliban who fired up at them or tried to launch a rocket or grenade at the bird. She nodded to short, stocky Andy, who was all of twenty years old.

Nike could feel Jackson's gaze burning two holes between her shoulder blades. He was watching her. Intently. Like a wolf on the prowl. Hunting *her*. Well, it would get him nowhere.

The brisk, early April morning was chilly. New snow had fallen overnight, leaving about six inches on the tarmac. There was barely light on the eastern horizon, the silhouette of the sharp mountain peaks highlighted. She had a dark green muffler wrapped around her neck and dangling down the front of her bulky dark green winter flight suit. As her fingers slowly froze, a mist came out of her mouth when she spoke to Andy.

"All here and accounted for?"

"Yes, ma'am. Ten-man A team." He consulted his papers

on a clipboard, and then he looked over at an approaching truck. "We'll be loading all the supplies and medicine in just a moment. We're on schedule."

After consulting her watch, Nike nodded. There was a timetable to keep and she was a punctual person by nature. "Very good, Sergeant. I'll do my walk around the helo while you're getting all those boxes on board."

"Of course, ma'am."

Scanning the area, Nike appreciated the towering mountains to the east of the small base. The village of Nar was two miles away. As the dawn grew brighter, she could see the mountains were still cloaked in heavy snow. Closer to the bottom, they appeared a dark blue color. Rubbing warmth into her arms, Nike wished she'd put on her flight jacket to keep her upper body protected against the gusting breeze coming off the mountains. She'd left the jacket on the seat in the cockpit of the helo. The sky was a deep cobalt blue above the backlit peaks. It would be a good hour before the sun, still hidden behind the peaks, would crest them. Nike noticed the last of the stars above her, twinkling and appearing close enough to reach out and touch. Most of these nap-of-the-earth flights were flown just above one hundred feet above the land. All flights departed early in the day when the dark-green-colored helicopter could be hidden in the mountain shadows from an ever-present enemy lurking below.

The canopied olive-green military truck backed up toward the chopper with Peters's hand signals to guide it. Two men hopped out of the cab once the truck halted. Nike went to the starboard side of her helo to begin her check of all flight surfaces.

"Want some company, Captain Alexander?"

Startled, Nike turned on the heel of her boot. Gavin

Jackson stood less than a foot away, a shy smile on his face. She hadn't heard him approach. *Stealth.* That was what hunter-killer A teams were all about: you must not be seen or heard in order to kill your target. Gulping convulsively, Nike pressed a hand to her neck. "You scared the hell out of me, Captain!"

"Oh, sorry," he said, shrugging. And then he brightened. "Call me Gavin when we're alone like this."

Scowling, Nike continued her slow walk along the two-engine helo. "I'll think about it," she said. Nike scanned the rivets in the plates for signs of wear or loosening. Craning her neck, she checked for hydraulic leaks from either of the two massive engines on each end of the bird.

Undeterred, Gavin fell into step with her. "Don't you think it's kismet that we've met twice in less than twenty-four hours?"

Giving him a long, dark look, Nike growled, "More like damnable karma if you asked me."

"Ouch."

"Oh, get over yourself, Captain Jackson." Nike faced him, her hands on her hips. He was about six foot two inches tall and it killed her to have to look *up* at him. His blue eyes were warm and inviting. Without thinking, her gaze fell to his smiling mouth. He had a very, very male mouth. And for a moment, Nike realized he would be a damned good kisser. But a lover? Just because he was a man didn't mean he automatically had the kind of maturity that Nike demanded. And why on earth was she even *thinking* along those lines with this rude dude?

Snorting, she jerked her gaze up. "Listen, hotshot, cool your jets. You're obviously starved for a warm female body, but remove me from your gun sights. I'm not interested."

Dark brows raising, Gavin backed off and held up his hands. "Whoa, Nike—"

"It's Captain Alexander to you." Nike flinched inwardly when she saw his cheeks beneath his beard go ruddy with embarrassment. He had enough humility to blush. Jackson wasn't really the ego-busting officer Nike had first thought. Hands still resting on her hips, she added with less acidity, "We have a job to do, Captain. I'll do mine and you do yours. All I have to do is fly your team into a village, drop you off and then I'm out of your life."

"That's not very optimistic," Gavin observed. Her face was a mask of wariness. And yet, he sensed a crack in that facade. Oh, it wasn't anything he could point to or see, but Gavin knew his little-boy expression had gotten to her. There wasn't a woman alive who wouldn't melt under that look. Of course, it wasn't really a ploy. Gavin was a little boy at heart when he could get away with it.

"War is *never* optimistic, Captain."

Shaking his head, Gavin said, "Now where did you pick up that attitude?"

"In Peru. Chasing druggies for three years. Give no quarter, take no quarter. That's my maxim, Captain."

"I like it," Gavin said, properly impressed. The corners of his mouth moved upward. "You're a brazen woman, Captain Alexander, and you make my heart beat faster."

Nike ignored the comment, though it secretly pleased her. She finished her inspection of her helo. Maybe he'd get the message and leave her alone. She felt Jackson approach and walk silently at her side. When she halted to touch the metal skin to inspect something more closely, he would wait without a word.

What kind of game was this? Nike thought for sure if she gave him "the look" that he'd disappear inside the helo. Nope. Not Gavin Jackson. He still had that thoughtful and curious expression on his face. His blue eyes gleamed with humor. In his business, there wasn't much to be merry about, yet, he looked amiable, approachable and drop-dead handsome.

"You know," Gavin said conversationally as she halted at the Plexiglas nose, "there isn't a man on this godforsaken base out in the middle of nowhere that isn't happy about BJS flying into town." He rubbed his hands. "An *all-woman* squadron. That's really something."

"We're black ops," she warned him. Jackson seemed absolutely joyous over the prospect of ten Apaches with twenty pilots and a mostly all-woman crew coming to this base. No wonder. "Not sex on legs."

"Ouch. Double ouch."

"Oh, give me a break, Captain. That's all you see us women as—bedding material." She moved around the nose to the port side of the helicopter.

"That's not fair."

A burst of sharp laughter erupted from Nike. "It's the truth, isn't it? Who said anything in life was fair?"

Nodding, Gavin moved with her, his hands behind his back and face thoughtful. "I see you as sharing more than just my bed."

"Oh sure," Nike said, eyeing him. She ran her cold fingers across the metal. Rivets would come loose under the constant shuddering and vibration of the blades turning. Never did she want any of these light aluminum panels to be ripped off midflight. It could cause a crash.

"No, seriously," Gavin pleaded. Leaning down, he caught her golden gaze. "I'm dying for some feminine companionship."

"Intelligent conversation with a woman? I like that."

The jeering in her tone made Gavin chuckle. "That's all I want, Captain Alexander—just a little conversation."

Nike shot him an I-don't-believe-you-for-a-second look and continued her walk around. As she leaned under the carriage, she checked the tires. The tread was thick and obviously new. That was good because when she landed this bird on rocky terrain, she didn't need a blowout. Tires had to be in top-notch condition.

"We have *nothing* in common except for this assignment, Captain Jackson."

"Are you so sure?"

Straightening to her full height, Nike grinned. "*Very* sure." He stood there with a quizzical expression on his features. And she had to admit, he had a nice face. She liked looking at him, with his wide brow and high cheekbones. He had a prominent nose and a solid chin hidden beneath the dark beard. His lips reminded her of those on a sculpted bust of Julius Caesar. They were his best attribute aside from his large, inquiring blue eyes. She found it tough to think of him as someone who could easily pull a trigger and kill someone if needed. Jackson just didn't seem like the killer type.

"Why don't you give me a chance to prove otherwise?" Gavin pleaded as they neared the rear ramp. He knew he could win her over. The men had just finished loading fifty boxes of supplies for the village. The truck fired up, the blue diesel smoke purling upward in thick, churning clouds. He halted. So did she. Nike seemed to be considering his challenge. *Good.*

Why did he want to engage her on any level? Hadn't he had enough with Laurie and her inability to compromise? Never mind he'd fallen head over heels in love with her. He'd been able to take her stubbornness in stride. Her ego was considerable and dominating like his. And that was what had broken them up. Two headstrong egos unable to bend. Laurie had brought out the worst in him. And he was as much at fault in the breakup as she was. Gavin felt men and women were equals—not one better than the other. Laurie, however, had felt that all women were inherently better than any man and that grated on Gavin, too.

"This attention is flattering but I'm busy," Nike told him with finality.

"Are you married?"

"That's none of your business, Captain." Nike glared at him. "Let's get this straight—I'm your pilot. I fly you in, drop your team off and leave. I come back with any supplies you radio in to ops. Nothing more or less. Got it?"

Sighing, Gavin said, "Yes, I got it. I wish it was otherwise, though." True, Nike had a helluva ego but didn't seem as stubborn as Laurie. "You're an interesting person. How many women have been flying against South American drug cartels?" He gave her a warm smile. "See? We really do have something to discuss. I'm kind of an interesting dude myself."

"Oh, I'm sure you think that," Nike said, laughing. She shook her head and moved up the ramp.

Gavin stood watching her pull on the helmet and get situated in the right-hand seat in the cockpit. Nodding to the load master, Gavin mounted the ramp.

His men were grinning expectantly at him as he made his way to his nylon seat right behind Nike. He held up his hands in a show of surrender and they all laughed. Gavin didn't mind making himself the target of fun or prodding. His team had had a two-week rest, and now they were going out again. This time, he hoped, to something less dangerous, but he wasn't sure of that.

The ramp groaned and rumbled upward until finally the hatch was shut with a loud clang. Darkness, except for the light coming in through the cockpit, made the inside of the helicopter gray. Gavin watched his men strap in, their weapons in hand, their faces belying their real thoughts. He prayed that as they approached Zor Barawul nearby Taliban soldiers wouldn't be firing RPGs at them as they came in for a landing. He knew from the premission briefing that the townspeople hated the Taliban. But were they pro-American? There was no way to know except to walk in, offer humanitarian aid and see what happened next. They had no script written for this newest idea by General Chapman.

After pulling on his helmet, Gavin plugged in the radio connection and heard Nike's honeyed voice as she talked with the base air controller for permission to lift off. She had already engaged one engine on the helo and then the other one. Gavin had found out at the briefing with his people that her usual copilot had food poisoning and there was no one to replace her. Nike was flying alone, which wasn't a good thing, but Gavin had seen it happen.

If they weren't wearing helmets, the noise created by the helicopter would be horrendous and would destroy their hearing in a short time. The bird shuddered and shook around him. The deck beneath his booted feet constantly shivered. If his men had any worry about a woman flying this huge, hulking transport helo a hundred feet off the earth, they didn't show it. Flying nap-of-the-earth took a helluva lot of skill. Gavin wondered how many hours she had of flight time. When Nike had finished her conversation with the tower, Gavin piped up, "Captain, how many hours do you have flying this bird?"

All his men heard the question, of course, because they,

too, had helmets on and were plugged in to the inter-cabin radio system. Gavin saw the load master at the far end turn and give him a questioning look. He also heard the explosion of laughter from Nike.

"Oh, let's see, Captain, I got my helo-driver's license at Disneyland in Orlando, Florida," she drawled. "Does that count?"

His men were guffawing in reaction, but no one could hear it over the noise of the vibrating helo around them. Jackson chuckled. "I feel better, Captain Alexander. So long as Mickey Mouse signed off on your pilot's license I feel safe and sound."

Jackson thought some of his men were going to fall out of their nylon seats they were laughing so hard. He joined them. And then he heard Nike joining their collective roar of laughter. She had a wonderful, husky tone and it made his body ache with need. What kind of magic did this Greek woman have over him?

"Actually," Nike said, chuckling, "it was Minnie Mouse who signed it. You have a problem with that?"

"No, not at all. Now, if Goofy had signed it, I'd be worried."

Even the load master was giggling in fits, his gloved hands closed over the fifty-caliber. Unaccountably, Gavin felt his spirits rise. If nothing else, Nike Alexander gave as good as she got. Even more to her credit, she could take a joke and come back swinging. Looking into the faces of his men, Gavin felt a warmth toward the woman pilot. Did Nike realize how much she'd just lifted everyone's spirits? Probably not. But he would tell her—alone—and thank her for being a good sport on a deadly mission.

"Okay, boys," Nike said, catching her breath, "let's get this show on the road. Sergeant, once we're airborne, lower the ramp and keep that .50 cal ready to shoot. We're not in Disneyland and where we're going, the bad guys are waiting. Hunker down, you're about to go on the wildest roller-coaster ride you've ever taken. I'm ready to rock...."

For the next fifty minutes, Nike's full concentration was winding between, around and down into one valley after another in the steep, rugged mountain range. When they roared past Do Bandi, another village, she knew they would soon be climbing steeply. Zor Barawul sat in a rich, fertile valley ringed by the snowy mountains. On the eastern side of those mountains lay the Pakistan border where Taliban hid. The valley was a well-known Taliban route. They boldly passed through it because the Afghan villagers could not fire on or challenge them. If they did, the Taliban would come in and kill men, women and children.

The sunlight shone in bright slats across the mountaintops as she brought the Chinook up steeply, pushing with throttles to the firewall to make it up and over the snowy slope that blurred beneath them. How badly Nike wanted a copilot to do all this other work, but that wasn't her luck today. Captain Emma Trayhern, the XO who was supposed to fly with her, had caught a nasty case of food poisoning and was laid low for the next twenty-four hours. Her CO, Dallas Klein, had faith in her to handle this mission all by herself. Helluva compliment, but Nike would have preferred a copilot, thank you very much. The sunlight made her squint even though she wore a pair of aviator's sunglasses. The bird rocked from one side to another as she aimed the nose downward at top speed and skimmed headlong down a steep, rocky slope and into another valley.

Nike could see herds of sheep and goats being tended by young boys here and there on the bright green valley floor. They would look up, wave as the CH-47 streaked by them. The herds of animals would flee in all directions as the noisy Chinook passed low overhead. Nike felt sorry for the young herders who would probably spend half a day gathering up their scattered herds. What she didn't want to see was yellow or red winking lights from below. That would mean the Taliban was firing a rocket up at them. *Not good.*

The mountains were coated with thick snow even in April. The lower slopes showed hopeful signs of greenery sprouting after enduring the fierce, cold Afghan winter. The helicopter vibrated heavily around Nike as she flew the bulky transport through the valley. Shoving the throttles once more to the firewall, she urged the helo up and over another mountain range and down into the next valley. And, as she glanced out her cockpit window, it was comforting to see an Apache helicopter with her women friends from BJS 60 flying several thousand feet above her, working their avionics to find the enemy below before they shot her Chinook out of the air. She might not have a copilot, but she had the baddest son-of-a-bitch of a combat helicopter shadowing her flight today. That made Nike smile and feel confident.

The village of Zor Barawul contained two hundred people and sat at the north end of a long, narrow valley that was sandwiched between the mountains. On the other side lay the border of Pakistan. As in all villages Nike had seen, the wealthy families had houses made of stone with wooden floors. Wood was usually scarce. Those less well-off had homes made of earth and mud with hard-packed dirt floors. Some who could afford it would have a few rugs over the earthen floor. Roofs were made from tin or other lightweight metals. The poorer families had thatched material on top.

As they passed over all kinds of homes, Nike felt the sweat beneath her armpits. Fear was always near since at any moment, they could be fired on. As she located the landing area, she ordered her load master to bring up the ramp. Moments later, she heard the grind and rumble of the ramp shutting. The ramp had to be up in order for her to land.

Nike brought the Chinook downward and gently landed it outside the village. The earth was bare and muddy. Nike let out a sigh of relief. They were down and had made it without incident. She powered down, shut off the engines and called to her friends in the Apache flying in large circles outside the village. This was Taliban-controlled territory and the Apache was using its television and infrared cameras to spot any possible enemy who might want to shoot at the Chinook after it had landed.

The whine of the engines ceased. The women in the Apache reported no activity and continued to circle about a mile from where she'd landed. Nike thanked them and signed off on the radio. The Apache would wait and escort her back to base as soon as everything was unloaded. Unstrapping the tight harness, she pulled the helmet off her head and stood. Andy had removed the fifty-caliber machine gun and set it to one side. He opened the ramp and it groaned down. Once the ramp lip rested on the muddy ground, Andy signaled the A team to dismount.

As she glanced to her left, Nike caught sight of Gavin. This time, he was grim-faced and not smiling. *Right.* He understood this was a very dangerous place. No one knew for sure how the villagers would respond to their landing. Bullets or butter? For a moment, Nike felt a twinge in her heart. Jackson looked so damned responsible and alert. This wasn't his first dance with the Afghan people. She saw the grimness reflected in the flat line of his mouth as he gathered his gear and slung it across his shoulder.

His other team members were already moving down the ramp. Several took the cargo netting off the many boxes and prepared to move them outside the helo. What were the people of this village thinking of their arrival? Were they scared? Thinking that the U.S. Army was going to attack them the way the Taliban did? When the Russians had invaded Afghanistan a decade before, that's exactly what they had done. People here justifiably had a long memory and would probably not trust the Americans, either.

"Hey, do these people know you're coming?" Nike called to Jackson.

"Yeah, we sent an emissary in here a week ago."

"So, they know you're on a mission of peace?"

He took the safety off his weapon and then slung it across his other shoulder. "That's right. It doesn't guarantee anything."

Worriedly, Nike looked out the end of the Chinook. She saw several bearded older men in turbans or fur hats walking toward them. "Well, they don't look real happy to see us."

Gavin glanced out the rear of the helo. "Oh. Those are the elders. They run the village. Don't worry, they always look that way. Survival is serious business out here."

"They're carrying rifles."

"They sleep with them."

Smiling a little over the comment, Nike walked down the ramp and stood next to him. "Do you ever not have a joke, Captain?"

Gavin grinned over at her. Nike's hair lay against her

brow, emphasizing her gold eyes. He heard the worry in her voice and reached out to squeeze her upper arm. "You care...."

Nike didn't pull away from where his hand rested on her arm. There was monitored strength to his touch and her flesh leaped wildly in response. Seconds later, his hand dropped away. "Oh, don't let it go to your swelled head, honcho."

"Hey, I like that nickname."

"It's wasn't a compliment."

Gavin chuckled. "I'll take it as such."

"Ever the optimist."

"I don't like the other choice, do you? Thanks for the wild ride, Captain." He gave her a salute and smiled. "How about a date when we get back off this mission?"

"That's not a good idea." Nike saw the regret in his deep blue eyes.

"Okay, I'll stop chasing you for now." Looking out the rear of the helo, Gavin said, "I'll be seeing you around, lioness."

She felt and heard the huskiness of his voice as he spoke the word. *Lioness.* Well, that was a nice compliment. Unexpected. Sweet. And her heart thumped in reaction. She hated to admit it but she really did care. But before she could open her mouth, he turned and walked nonchalantly down the ramp and into the dangerous world of the Taliban-controlled village.

Suddenly, Nike was afraid for Gavin and his team. The ten elders approached in their woolen cloaks, pants and fur hats to ward off the morning coldness. They looked unwelcoming and grim.

Well, it wasn't as if she could help him and she had to get back to base. A part of her didn't want to leave Gavin.

Nike looked up and saw the Apache continuing its slow circuit at about three thousand feet. *Time to move.* Grabbing her helmet, she gave Andy a gesture that told him to lift up the ramp. He nodded. As soon as they were airborne, he'd lower the ramp once more and keep watch with his hands on that machine gun.

Settling into her seat, Nike pulled on her helmet, plugged it back in and made contact with the Apache once more.

"Time to boogie outta here, Red Fox One. Over."

"Roger, Checkerboard One. All quiet on the western front here."

Nike chuckled and twisted around. The ramp ground upward and locked against the bird, causing the whole helo to shudder. Andy gave her a thumbs-up and put on his helmet. All was well. Turning around, Nike began to flip switches and twist buttons. As soon as she was ready to turn on the engines, one at a time, she'd get harnessed up for the harrowing one-hundred-foot-high flight back to base. It wasn't something Nike looked forward to.

And then, her world came to an abrupt halt. A glaring red light began to blink back at her on the console—the forward engine light. Scowling, she flipped it off and on. *Red. Damn.* That meant either a problem with the engine or a screw-up with the light itself. Nike could do nothing at this point.

"Red Fox One, I have a red light for the forward engine. I can't go anywhere. Can you contact base to get a helo out here with a couple of mechanics? Until then, I'm grounded. I'll radio Operations and get further instructions from them. Over."

"Bad news, Checkerboard One. Stay safe down there. Out."

Well, it didn't take long for Nike to get her answers. Major Dallas Klein, who was in ops, answered her.

"Stay where you are. We can't get a mechanic team out until tomorrow morning. Stick with Captain Jackson and his team. Your load master will remain with the helicopter. In the meantime, go with the A team. We'll be in touch by radio when we know the time of arrival to your location. Over."

Great. Nike scowled and responded. "Roger. Over and out."

Now what? She gestured for Andy to come forward because he had not been privy to what was going on. Shaking her head, Nike felt a sense of dread combined with unexplainable elation. She was stuck here with Jackson, who clearly would be delighted with her company. *Double damn.*

Chapter 3

Jackson walked toward village elders. The knot of men stood watching them. But before he could talk with them, Nike appeared at his shoulder, her face set and disappointed.

"What's wrong?" he asked, anchoring to a halt.

"My helo has engine failure and I've got orders to stay the night here with you and your team. My load master will remain with the bird. A mechanic team will be flown out to fix it tomorrow morning."

She didn't seem too happy about the news but joy threaded through Gavin. "Engine failure." He tried to sound disappointed for her. "Sorry about that, Captain Alexander."

Nike tried to avoid his powerful stare and glanced over at the knot of elders. They were a sour-looking bunch. Every one of them wore a deep, dark scowl of suspicion. She returned her attention to Jackson. "Let's look at the positives. This engine failure could have happened en route. We're damned lucky to have landed before the problem."

"And here I thought you were a doom-and-gloom pessimist." Jackson grinned and desperately wanted this moment alone with her, but the elders had to be properly greeted.

Nike shook her head and muttered, "Jackson, you're a piece of work."

He smiled quickly and then resumed his serious demeanor toward the elders. "Thank you."

"It wasn't a compliment."

"As always, I'll take anything you say as a positive."

"Get real," she gritted between her teeth so that only he could hear her. On either side of them, the team had fanned out, hands on their weapons but trying not to appear threatening to the elders.

"Do me a favor?" Gavin said.

"Depends upon what it is."

"These elders have strict laws regarding their women. I'll be speaking to them in Pashto. They may have a problem with you not wearing a *hijab,* or scarf, on your head. That scarf is a sign of honoring their Moslem beliefs. So, if it comes to pass that someone hands you a scarf, wear it."

Nike nodded. "No problem."

"Thanks, I needed that."

"Judging from their looks, you're going to need more than a scarf on my head to turn this situation into a positive, honcho."

Gavin said nothing. Nike took a step back, partly hidden by his tall, lean frame. The elders looked aged, their weathered faces deeply lined. Their skin was tobacco-brown, resembling leather, because of their tough outdoor life. Nike knew the elements at the top of the world in this mountain chain were unforgiving and brutal. Villages along the border had no electricity, no sewers and sometimes little water. These rugged Afghan people eked out a living raising goats and sheep. At this altitude, poppy crops wouldn't grow because the season was too short. Winter came early and stayed late. Nike had found out through the weather officer at BJS ops that snow started in September and lasted sometimes into June. That was why they couldn't grow crops and relied heavily on their animals for a food source.

The elders had good reason to be serious-looking, their hands hidden in the sleeves of their woolen robes, chins held high and their dark eyes assessing the A team. These proud and fiercely independent Afghan people had few resources. Beneath their threadbare woolen clothing, Nike saw the thinness of all the elders. There wasn't a fat one in the group. Their leanness was probably due to the hardships of living in such a rocky, inhospitable place. She felt compassion and respect toward them, not animosity.

Gavin had been given an in-depth briefing on Zor Barawul before arriving at the village. Photos had been taken and the elders were identified in them. He recognized the chief elder, Abbas, who separated himself from the group. He was in his sixties and every inch like his name, which meant "angry lion" in Pashto. They approached each other like two competing football-team captains staring one another down. Tension sizzled in the cold morning air between the two groups of men. Walking forward, Gavin extended his hand to Abbas, who wore a dark brown turban and cloak. The man's face was as narrow and thinned as a starving lion's, horizontal lines deeply carved across his broad brow. Gashes slashed down on either side of his pursed lips. Ordinarily, the Afghan custom of greeting was to shake hands and then kiss each other's cheeks as a sign of friendship.

That wasn't going to happen here. Gavin fervently hoped that Abbas would at least shake his extended hand. The elder glared at him and then down at his hand. No, that wasn't going to happen, either. Gavin pressed his right hand over his heart, bowed referentially and murmured, *"Salaam-a-laikam."* This meant "peace be with you," and was a greeting given no matter if the person were Moslem or of some other faith. It was a sign of respect and of the two people meeting on common ground.

Scowling, Abbas touched his chest where his heart lay and murmured, *"Wa alaikum assalam wa rahmatu Allah,"* in return. That meant "And to you be peace together with God's mercy."

Gavin could see that Abbas was surprised by his sincere and knowledgeable greeting. His scowl eased and his voice became less gruff. "We told your emissary last week, Captain Jackson, that we did *not* want you to come to our village. The Kabul government has always ignored us. There is no reason you should be here at their invitation. If the Taliban finds out we are dealing with the Americans, they will come back here and kill more of my people. We are a tribe and as such, do not recognize the government as having any power or control over our lives," Abbas said in Pashto, his arms remaining tightly wrapped against his chest.

Halting, Gavin allowed his hand to drop back to his side. *"Sahibji,"* he began in Pashto, "we do not come as representatives of the Kabul government. I realize you do not acknowledge them. The American people have donated all of this—" he turned and swept his hand toward the stacked boxes "—as respect for your tribe. Americans believe in peace and when they found out that your children needed help, they sent these boxes of medicine to you." Gavin kept his voice sincere. "There is also food and blankets for your people, if you will accept their heartfelt generosity."

Gavin knew that Afghan people, when given a sincere gift, would never forget the heart-centered gesture and would be friends for life with the givers. They were a remarkable warrior class who judged others on their loyalty and honor. They held an ancient set of codes based upon Islamic belief and here, in these mountains, the villagers practiced these morals and values to this day. That was one of the reasons the Russians had never been able to break the spirit of these proud people. The more they tried to destroy the Afghan tribal culture, the more stubborn the people became. Gavin felt General Chapman's operation to win the hearts and minds of these people, one village at a time along the border, was much wiser and more humane. Gavin knew the Afghans would respond to honest gifts given from the heart, for they, above all, were a heart-centered people.

Abbas's thick black-and-gray brows lifted slightly as he looked longingly toward the boxes. Then, his mouth curled as he swung his gaze back to the captain. "And for this you want what?"

Shrugging, Gavin said, "The opportunity to earn your friendship over time. Judge us on a daily basis and allow us to earn your respect." He knew that the Afghan people were a proud people and that they were slow to give their trust. It was earned by deeds alone—not by any words, but actions.

"I have families who are sick and ailing," Abbas said abruptly. "Even if there is medicine, there is no doctor. So what good is all of this?"

Gavin turned to his medic, Staff Sergeant Neal Robles.

"This is Sergeant Robles. He is my paramedic and one level below a medical doctor. We have brought him to help your people. We are here on a strictly humanitarian mission. We are not here to cause stress or fighting."

Grunting, Abbas lifted his chin a little higher. He stroked his salt-and-pepper beard. Looking over at the paramedic, he demanded, "And this man can do what?"

"He can give vaccinations to all your children. Many Afghan children die unnecessarily of diseases and our vaccinations can stop that. He can examine a male and treat him accordingly. We have brought antibiotics, as well."

At that, Abbas's brows lifted in surprise. Hope flared in his narrowed eyes.

Gavin saw his response. Abbas knew antibiotics were as valuable a commodity as opium made from the poppy fields of southern Afghanistan. The elder understood, thankfully, that antibiotics could save a life. But in this remote village, there was no way to get them nor was there the help of a doctor to dispense the lifesaving drug. Gavin was sure that Abbas had seen any number of children, men and women die of ailments that could have been stopped and turned around by antibiotics. "Sergeant Robles will train a man and a woman whom you suggest to use the antibiotics that we will supply to you. Your village will always have them on hand from now on." Gavin could see the surprise and then the gratefulness in the man's narrowed dark eyes.

Abbas heard the elders of the village whispering excitedly over the officer's last statement. Turning, he saw them eagerly nod over receiving such a gift. His tribe had suffered severely for years beneath the Kabul government, the Russians and now, the Taliban. Drilling a look into the captain, Abbas growled, "My people have died without the help of our own government. They do not care whether we exist. If not for a Sufi brother and sister who are medical doctors who visit our village twice a year, many more would have died." He jammed a long, thin index finger down at the hard brown earth where he stood.

"The United States of America is trying to change that," Gavin told him in a persuasive tone. "We are here on a mission of mercy." He walked toward the boxes, printed in English and Pashto. "Come and see. This is not the Kabul government nor my government. This is from the American people who do not like to see anyone's children die. Look at the gifts from my people to your villagers. There is clothing, blankets, food and medicine. All we ask is to be able to distribute it and have our medic help those who ask for medical attention."

Abbas walked commandingly over to the bounty, his lean shoulders squared, head held at a proud angle. He reached out with long brown hands and placed them on the tops of several of the cardboard boxes. Walking around the fifty cartons, he stopped, read the Pashto lettering on one and then moved on. The rest of the elders came to his side at his gesture. Gavin watched the group of men carefully read each label and check out the gifts.

Gavin turned and to Nike spoke quietly, "Listen, I need a favor. There are women here who need medical attention. Abbas isn't about to let Robles touch any Moslem female since it's against their religion. Can I volunteer you to help him?"

"But I don't have any medical training," Nike whispered.

"Doesn't matter. Robles will teach you the basics."

She saw the pleading in his eyes. "I don't want to hurt anyone with my lack of experience."

"Don't worry, that won't happen."

Abbas strode over and gave Gavin a brusque nod of acceptance. "Allah is good. The gifts are indeed welcome, Captain Jackson. *Shukria,* thank you."

"You're welcome, *malik sahib,*" Gavin murmured, touching his heart and bowing his head respectfully to the elder.

Mouth quirking, Abbas looked directly at Nike and jabbed a finger toward her. "And this is the woman who will help Dr. Robles?"

Gavin didn't want to correct the elder. To do so would be a sign of disrespect. Besides, it would humiliate Abbas in front of the others and he had no wish to destroy what little trust he had just forged between them. "Yes, sir. Captain Nike Alexander will assist Dr. Robles, if you wish. With your permission, she will care for the women and girls of your village."

"I wish it to be so," Abbas said in a gruff tone. "My wife, Jameela, will bring her a *hijab* to wear over her head. She must respect Islam." He folded his arms across his narrow chest. "You are welcome to remain here and help my people, Captain Jackson. We are a peaceful tribe of sheep- and goat-herders. I will have my second-in-command, Brasheer, help you." He eyed Nike. "This woman is not allowed among your men. She will remain at our home. My wife will give her a room and she will remain in the company of women and children only."

"Of course," Gavin murmured, and he explained that Nike would be a transiting visitor because the helo was down. "You are most gracious," he told Abbas, giving him a slight bow of acknowledgment. "We would like to stay as long as you need medical help."

"I approve. Captain, you shall honor me by being my guest at every meal. We will prepare a room in our house for you. Your men will be housed at the other homes, fed, and given a place to sleep."

"Thank you, *malik sahib.* You are more than generous. We hope our stay improves the health of your people." Gavin could see the hope burning in the old man's eyes. As an elder, he carried the weighty responsibility for everyone in his village. It wasn't something Gavin himself would want to carry. Abbas must realize what these gifts would do to help his people. And he knew he was weighing Taliban displeasure over it, too. The Taliban would punish the village for taking the offered supplies and the old man took a surprising risk. With such humanitarian aide, this village might become less fearful of the Taliban and provide information to stop the terrorists from crossing their valley in the future. For now, no one in the villages gave away that information.

Gavin finished off the details of where the boxes would be taken and stored. All his men could speak Pashto. Robles was as fluent as Gavin and that would work in their favor. The other elders took over the management of the boxes while his A team became the muscle to carry the cartons toward the village.

Gavin watched as the elders left, parading the groups of carriers and boxes back into their village like conquering heroes. "Do you know any Pashto?" he asked Nike.

"I have problems with English sometimes and I'm Greek, remember?"

"So, I guess that's a no." Grinning, Gavin felt the tension melting off his tense shoulders. Just looking into Nike's gold eyes made him hungry for her again. Black curls framed her face and Gavin had to stop himself from reaching out and threading his fingers through that dark, shining mass. "Pashto isn't that difficult. Most villagers don't speak

English. I'll get one of my other men to help interpret from a distance. You can always go outside the home and talk to him out in the street and he can translate. He won't be allowed in where there is a female."

"That sounds like a workable strategy." She narrowed her eyes on Gavin. "So how did it go with Abbas? He looked like he'd just won the lottery when he read some of the labels on that shipment."

Gavin laughed a little while keeping alert. Taliban came through this valley all the time, and he knew that with an American A team here, word would get out to their enemy. "The elders' main concern is the health of their people. We've done this type of mission in southern Afghanistan for the last year and it was a great success. The key is in establishing trust with the Afghans."

Nike nodded and noticed how Jackson remained alert. She was glad the .45 pistol was strapped to her left leg. And wearing a bulletproof vest gave her a strong sense of protection. She hated wearing the chafing vest, but this was Dodge City and bullets could fly at any time. "I thought I saw tears in his eyes. He kept stroking the tops of the boxes that contained the antibiotics. It reminds me of a Greek proverb—*Upon touching sand may it turn to gold.* Only this time, his gold is the lifesaving drugs for his people."

Grimly, Gavin agreed and said, "I'm sure he's seen many of his people die terrible, suffering deaths that could have been avoided if they'd only had antibiotics available to them."

"Pnigese s'ena koutali nero," she agreed softly in Greek.

Cocking his head, Gavin said, "What did you just say?"

"You drown in a teaspoon of water. Another one of my

Greek sayings I was raised with. It's the equivalent to your saying that for want of a nail the horse's shoe is lost, and for want of a shoe the horse is lost, and for want of a horse, the battle is lost." She held up her finger. "Antibiotics are a small thing, but in his world, they're huge," Nike said. "Why was Abbas pointing at me earlier?"

"His wife, Jameela, will bring you a *hijab* to wear. Just be grateful to her for the gesture. Moslem women always wear the *hijab* any time they're outside their home. In Arabic it means *covering* or *concealing*." His mouth pulled into a devilish grin. "The best part is Abbas inviting us to stay at his home. The men and women are always separated. You'll be on the women's side of the house and have your own room. You'll also eat separately, too."

"That's a little strict."

"I agree, but we have to be aware of their religious laws. Afghans see that as a sign of respect. And respect can, we hope, earn us friendship with them."

Nike said, "Okay, boss, I can do it. Not exactly military issue, but in black ops you have to be flexible."

"Good. Come on, I see a woman coming toward us. She's got a red *hijab* in hand, so that must be Jameela."

When Gavin placed his hand beneath her elbow, Nike was surprised. She felt a sense of protection emanating from him. It was like a warm blanket surrounding her and she couldn't protest the nice gesture. The entire village, it seemed, had come out to view the boxes. Indeed, word had traveled fast. Women, men and children stood as the elders marched past them with the A team carrying some of the boxes. There was crackling excitement and expectation in the air.

"Women are pretty well hidden here from the outer world. When they're inside their homes they don't have to wear a burka or *hijab*. And there's real power among the women. They treat one another like sisters. Even though you may think the women have it bad, they really run the place. They have a lot of power in the household and in the village decisions in general. The women learned a long time ago to stick together as a unit. United they stand and divided they fall. Woman power is strong among the Afghan women and I think you'll enjoy being a part of it," Gavin told her conversationally as they walked toward Jameela. The elder's wife wore a black burka. The black wool robe swathed her from her head to her shoes. A crosshatch opening revealed her cinnamon-colored eyes.

"Don't expect me to wear one of those things," Nike warned him with a growl. "All the women are dressed like her. I'm not going to wear a burka. I'll stay in my uniform."

"They won't ask you to don a burka, so don't worry. Little girls don't start wearing them until around age seven. Until then, they've still got their freedom from the burka."

Nike grumbled, "I have a really hard time thinking any woman would be happy wearing a burka."

"Try to be gracious and don't stir up trouble with Jameela—she's the chieftain's wife. There's an unspoken hierarchy here in these villages. She's boss of the women and children. Jameela wields a lot of power even though she's hidden under that burka. Don't ever underestimate her position and authority. In reality, the women have equal power to any of these men. It may not appear to be like that, but from what I've seen, it is."

"*All* women are powerful," Nike reminded him. She felt his hand slip away as they walked to meet the tall, thin woman swathed in the black wool robe.

"No argument from me." And then Gavin turned slightly, gave her a wink and added teasingly, "Especially you…"

Nike had no time to retort. She felt heat rising in her face. Gavin chuckled with delight. Focusing on Jameela, Nike searched the woman's spice-brown eyes between the fabric crosshatch. It was Jameela's only opening into the outside world. Nike felt at odds with the woman, who stood about five foot six inches tall. Only her hands, reddened and work-worn, told Nike of her hard, unrelenting life.

Gavin bowed in respect to Jameela and offered the Islamic greeting to her as they halted about six feet from one another. Jameela whispered softly the return greeting to Gavin and to Nike, who bowed slightly, pressed her hand to heart and said, *"Salaam."* She didn't know what else they said to one another, but at one point, Jameela leaned forward and gave Nike the *hijab.* She made some gestures indicating she should wrap it around her head.

Nike gave her a friendly smile and put it on. Once the knotted scarf was in place, Jameela's eyes crinkled as if she were smiling. Perhaps she was grateful to Nike for honoring their customs. Not being able to see another person's body language or their facial expressions was highly disconcerting. Nike realized in those minutes how much she truly assessed a person through nonverbal means. Jameela remained a mystery to her.

"I speak…English…little…" Jameela said haltingly to Gavin and Nike, opening her hands as if to apologize.

Nike was delighted and grinned. She saw Gavin smile and nod.

"Where did you learn English?" Gavin asked her politely. He knew that Jameela shouldn't be talking to him. Under the circumstances, he felt it was all right but not something to be done more than once outside her home.

"When I was little, my parents lived in Kabul. I was taught English at a Christian missionary school." Shrugging her small shoulders beneath the burka, Jameela laughed shyly. "Coming out here, I could not practice it. So, I am very poor at speaking your language, but I will try."

"Thank you, *memsahib,*" Gavin told her quickly in Pashto. "My friend, Captain Nike Alexander—" he gestured toward her "—is here to help the women and children. Perhaps you could interpret for her? She does not know Pashto."

Jameela nodded in deference toward Nike. "Of course, Captain, I would be happy to. Please, apologize to her that I speak broken English?"

Gavin nodded. "Of course, *memsahib,* but you speak English very well. I know Captain Alexander will be grateful for your English and translation help. Thank you."

Jameela bowed her head slightly, her long hands clasped in front of her. Nike could have sworn the Afghan woman blushed, but it was hard to tell with the burka like a wall between them.

"You are the first Americans to come here," Jameela told Gavin in a softened tone. "There are Sufi twin brother and sister medical doctors, Reza and Sahar Khan, who visit us once every six months. The Sufis are heart-centered and they help us greatly. The Khan twins travel from the northern border of Afghanistan and follow it all the way to the south helping the villages along the way. Then, they turn around in their Jeep and come back north to do it all over again. We bless them. The Sufis are a branch of Islam who are dedicated to compassionate love toward all, no matter what their beliefs."

"Yes, I'm aware of the Sufis' nature," Gavin told her in Pashto. "I'm also aware that the Taliban hate them. The

Sufis practice peace at all costs and the Taliban has been known to kill them."

Jameela nodded sadly. "That is so, Captain Jackson. But Doctors Reza and Sahar Khan are welcomed by all our villages along the border, regardless. We greet them and bring them into our villages on two white horses. We place flower wreaths around their necks and sing their praises. That is our custom of honoring their courage to care for us regardless of the personal danger they place themselves in. They have saved many of our people over the years."

"I've heard the Khans mentioned by other villagers," Gavin said. "I hope one day to meet them. They're heroic people and give the Sufis a good name around the world for their courage and generosity."

Jameela hesitated and then said, "My husband is afraid Americans coming here will invite another Taliban attack upon us. Surely you know this?"

Nodding, Gavin said gently, "I understand that. We hope to win his trust over time, *memsahib*. And my team will be in your valley here to protect you from the Taliban. Our mission is to show that the American people are generous and care, especially for those who are sick."

Jameela looked toward the sky. "Allah be praised, Captain. You have no idea the prayers I have said daily to Him, asking for more help. If you stay in our valley then the Taliban won't attack us. Our Sufi brother and sister constantly travel. We understand they can only visit us twice a year." She gestured gracefully toward the village. "Captain Alexander, you will come with me, and I will put you to work. Captain Jackson, you may join your men."

"Of course," Gavin said, and he winked over at Nike. "I'll catch up with you later. And I'll have Sergeant Robles alerted to your requests. Just relax. It will all work out."

Nike wasn't so sure, but said nothing. She didn't want this humanitarian mission scuttled because of her lack of medical knowledge. As she walked with Jameela, she said, "Are your duties the same as your husband's in running this village?" Nike knew little of the Afghan culture and didn't want to make a gaffe. Better to ask than to assume.

Jameela nodded. "My duty first is to my husband and our family. After that, I am looked upon to provide leadership to the women of the village in all matters that concern us."

"I see," Nike said. She suddenly had a humorous thought that couldn't be shared with Jameela. Wearing a bright red scarf, a dark green flight suit and a pistol strapped to her waist, she must look quite a sight! The women of the BJS would laugh until it hurt if they could see her in her new fashion garb. Still, Nike wanted to fit in, and she would allow the course of the day to unfold and teach her. Often, prejudices and misunderstandings from one country or culture to another caused tension and she would not want to create such problems.

As Nike followed Jameela down the muddy, rutted street, she was struck by the young children playing barefoot on such a cold April morning. The children's clothes were threadbare with many patches sewn in the fabric. They shouted and danced. Their gazes, however, were inquisitive and they stared openly at Nike. What an odd combination she wore—a man's trousers with the prescribed headdress of a Moslem woman. Fired with curiosity, the group followed them down the middle of the wide street where mud and stone homes sat close to one another.

As Nike smiled at the children, she regretted not knowing Pashto. Their eyes were button-bright and shining. Little girls and boys played with one another just as they would in the States or in her homeland of Greece. But then, as she glanced farther up the street, her heart saddened. A little girl of about six years old stood on crutches near a large stone home. The child had only one leg. Nike remembered that damnable land mines covered this country. Most of them had been sown by Russians, but of late, it had been the Taliban, too. Had this child stepped on one? Nike's heart contracted. There was no doctor here to help her. No painkillers. No antibiotics. How had she survived?

"Jameela? That little girl over there? Who is she?"

"My youngest daughter, Atefa. Why do you ask?"

Gulping, Nike hoped she hadn't made a fatal mistake by asking. "I…uh…she's missing one leg. Did she step on a land mine?"

"Yes, as a four-year-old." Jameela's voice lowered with anguish as she pointed outside the village and to the east. "Afghan national soldiers laid land mines everywhere outside our village two years ago. They wanted to stop the Taliban from coming through our valley." Choked anger was evident in her quiet tone.

"How did Atefa *ever* survive such a terrible injury?" Nike asked softly.

"Allah's will," Jameela murmured. "Everyone said she would die, but I did not believe it. Dr. Reza Khan and his sister, Sahar, found her near the road where it happened. They saved her life and brought her to the village in their Jeep. Then, we had Farzana, our wise woman, tend her with the antibiotics the doctor left. Also, Dr. Sahar knows much about herbs and she directed Farzana how to use them."

"That's an amazing story," Nike said, her voice thick with unshed tears. People like the Sufi medical doctors inspired her. She'd never heard of Sufis or that they were Moslem. Nike decided she was very ignorant of Moslems in general. What if the Sufi doctors hadn't been on the road driving by when Atefa had been injured? Nike watched as the child hobbled toward them on carved wooden crutches. "She's so pretty, Jameela. What does her name mean?" Nike wondered.

"It means *compassion* in our language. Little did I know when my husband and I chose that name for her that she would, indeed, bring exactly that to our family and village. My husband wants her to go to a school in Pakistan when she's old enough. He feels Allah has directed this because she was saved by Sufis."

Atefa had dark brown, almond-shaped eyes; her black hair was long and drawn into a ponytail at the back of her head. She wore a black woolen dress that hung to her ankle; her foot was bare. To Nike, she looked like a poor street urchin. But then, as she scanned the street, she realized all the children shared in the same impoverished appearance as Atefa. The children were clean, their clothes were washed, their skin was scrubbed clean, their hair combed, but this was a very poor village.

"Maybe," Nike told Jameela, briefly touching her arm for a moment, "there is something that might be done to help Atefa before she goes to her school."

Chapter 4

"How are things going?" Gavin asked as Nike finished ensuring her helo was protected for the night. She'd just sent Andy into the village to grab a bite to eat at Abbas's house before staying with the bird during the coming darkness.

She turned, surprised by Gavin's nearness. The man walked as quietly as a cat, never heard until he wanted to be. His cheeks were ruddy in the closing twilight. "Doing okay." She held up her gloved hands. "Today, I became 'Dr. Nike' to the women and children in the village." She laughed. The look in his narrowed eyes sent her heart skipping beats. She stood with her back against the Chinook, for the metal plates still exuded the warmth of the sun from the April day.

"Yeah, Robles said you were doing fine. He's proud that you can give vaccinations. You're a fast study."

Nike grinned. "I had to be! I wasn't given a choice."

The jagged mountain peaks became shadowed as the sun slid below the western horizon.

"From all accounts, old Abbas seems to be satisfied with our efforts."

"Him." Nike rolled her eyes. "That old man is married to a woman thirty years his junior!"

"That's not uncommon out here," Gavin said. "Wives die in childbirth and there's no medical help to change the outcome. The man will always marry again." He grimaced. "And let's face it, there are many widows around and they need a man in order to survive out here."

"Jameela said Abbas has had two other wives before her. Both died in childbirth." Shaking her head, Nike muttered, "Things were bad in Peru, too. BJS did a lot of flying into the jungle villages to deliver health care when we weren't chasing druggies. This place is a lot worse."

Gavin enjoyed being close to Nike. About six inches separated them and he wished he could close the gap. The best he could do was keep them talking. "These people deserve our help. You look kind of pretty in that red *hijab*. Do you like wearing it?"

"No, but I respect their traditions. At least Abbas didn't demand I climb into one of those burkas."

"Indoors, the women wear more casual clothes and no *hijab*," Gavin told her. "It's just when they go out in the community that they put on the burka or *hijab*."

"That robe looks like a prison to me," Nike muttered. "I asked Jameela today what she thought of the burka and she liked it. I couldn't believe it."

"In their culture, most women accept that their body and face are to be looked upon only by their husbands. The way the men figure it, if the woman is hidden, she's not a temptation to others."

"Why don't their husbands show some responsibility for what's between their legs? Then a woman would be safe to wear whatever she wants."

"Yeah, I can't disagree with your logic, but that's not the way their world turns, and sometimes we have to fit in, not try to change it."

Nike felt the coldness coming off the mountains in the evening breeze. "I feel absolutely suffocated by their culture's attitudes toward women. You don't find an Afghan woman flying a combat helicopter."

"No doubt." Gavin saw her put her hands beneath the armpits of her jacket to keep them warm. He took a step forward and allowed his heavily clothed body to contact hers. Her eyes widened for a moment. "I'll keep you warm," he soothed.

"Right now, I'm so damned cold I'm not going to protest."

Chuckling, Gavin continued to look around. "Things seem to be quiet. I've been working with Abbas most of the day. You know, he won't admit that the Taliban comes through their village, but we have satellite photos as proof."

"Is he pro-Taliban? Or just afraid of them like everyone else?" Nike absorbed the heat from his woolen Afghan clothes. For a moment, she wondered what it would be like to slide her hands beneath the folds and place her hands against his well-sprung chest. It was a forbidden thought, but tantalizing, nonetheless.

"I'm pretty sure he's afraid of them. There aren't many village chieftains or sheiks who get in bed with the devil and the Taliban is all of that," Gavin said, his mouth quirking. "He told me that the Taliban came in here and ordered their girls' school shut down. He's a man of education, and he didn't like being ordered to do that. Abbas continues to teach the girls and women of his village behind closed doors in defiance of their orders. He's a man of strong principles and morals. He believes women deserve education just as much as any man. And Abbas is enlightened compared to other village leaders."

"He was a teacher?" Nike found that inspiring for a man who lived in such a rugged, isolated area.

"Abbas was born here in this village. His father sent him to Kabul for higher schooling. He graduated with a degree in biology. When Abbas returned home, he helped the village breeding programs so that their sheep produced better wool. That helps to raise their economy because better wool demands a higher price at market. And he increased goat-milk output. He's done a lot in the region and he's respected by everyone because of this."

"Wow, I'd never have guessed. No wonder he's the head elder."

"Looks *are* deceiving." Gavin watched the high clouds across the valley turn a dark pink as the sun set more deeply below the western mountains. "He's carrying a lot of loads on his shoulders, Nike. Abbas takes his responsibilities as leader seriously. He's got a lot of problems and few ways to resolve them. When I asked him about medical and health help from the Afghan government, he got angry. Over the years, he's made many trips to the capital to urge them to bring out a health team every three months to these border villages, but he could never get them to agree to it. And Afghan people are superindependent. They really have a tough time looking at a centralized government to rule over them."

"That's awful that the politicians in Kabul wouldn't help

these people. Can you imagine *that* happening in the USA or Greece? There would be a helluva uprising."

"Abbas doesn't accept his government's lack of care," Gavin said. "When you realize Afghanistan is cobbled together out of about four hundred different clans or tribes, you can see why they wouldn't place trust in a Kabul government. Our job is to try and persuade Abbas that his own government does want to work with him."

"How are you going to convince him Kabul's listening and willing to pitch in some medical help out here in the border area?"

"I told Abbas that the report I write up regarding our visit will be given to the health minister of the government. This minister is trying hard to change old, outdated policies. I pointed out to Abbas other border villages south of him already have intervention, supplies and funds on a routine schedule from Kabul."

"Does he believe you?"

"No, but over time he will."

"And you and your team will stay here four weeks?"

"Yes. From the satellite photos, we know that the Taliban uses the north end of this valley twice a month. We've set up to be here when they try to cross it a week from now."

"And then what?" Nike grew afraid for Gavin and his team.

He shrugged. "Do what we're good at—stopping them cold in their tracks and denying them access across this valley."

"What will Abbas do?"

"I don't know. He knows if we stop the Taliban from crossing, they could take revenge on this village. This is what Abbas is worried about."

"He's right about that." Nike leaned against Gavin a

little more. The dusk air had a real bite to it. His arms came around and bracketed her. For a moment, she questioned her silent body language. Why had she done this? Something primal drove her like a magnet to this military man. Fighting herself, Nike finally surrendered to the moment. She had been too long without a man in her life, and she was starved for male contact. Yet, what message did this send to Gavin? Was he reading her correctly or assuming? Unsure, Nike remained tense in his embrace.

"Comfy?" he teased quietly. Surprised by Nike's unexpected move, Gavin hungrily savored her nearness. He had wrapped his arms around her but resisted pressing her tightly against himself. Right now, just the fact she'd allowed this kind of intimate contact was enough of a gift. Even though they sparred like fighters in a ring, he'd seen something in her gold eyes that he could never quite accurately read. Maybe this was the result of that smoldering look he'd seen banked in her expression. Only time and patience would tell.

"Yes, thank you."

Gavin wasn't about to do anything stupid. She had given herself to him in a way that he'd never entertained. Maybe it was the pink beauty of the clouds across the valley that had inspired her in this wonderful moment.

"What are you going to do here?" Nike asked.

"We know from satellite reconnaissance that the Taliban uses the north end of this valley at the new moon, when it's darkest. We'll be intercepting them if they try it next week."

"There's only ten of you. There could be a hundred or more fighters crossing that border and coming down into this valley."

"Are you worried?" Gavin ventured.

"Any sane person would be."

Laughing quietly, Gavin closed his eyes for a moment and simply absorbed the curves of Nike's womanly body against him. What an unexpected reward. It was precious in his world of ongoing war and violence. A sweet reminder of peace, of love and nurturance. Something he hadn't experienced for a long time. "You're right," he admitted. "But we look at it this way—our base camp where you're assigned isn't that far away. We have BJS here with Apache helos to help us out if we're attacked. We know you gals will hightail it in our direction and drop the goods on the Taliban so we'll survive to fight them another day."

"I have never met such an optimist," Nike said.

"I don't like the other possibility. Do you?" Gavin asked. He watched the clouds reflect pinkish light across the valley. In the background, he could hear the bleating of sheep and goats from their pens within the village. At dusk, boys tending the herds brought them into the village to protect them against wild animals and roving Taliban. Both two- and four-legged predators were always hungry for village meat.

Feeling uneasy and caring too much for Gavin even though she didn't want to, Nike said, "No, I don't like the alternative. This is a dangerous mission."

"Yeah, it is. We're out in the wilderness and the bad guys are right over that mountain to the east of us." He lifted his gloved hand to point at the darkened peaks. Bringing his hand down, he wrapped his arms around her once more. "Don't worry, we know our job, Nike. We've already survived a year here."

"And you're on your second tour."

Hearing the flatness in her tone, Gavin nodded. "We're slowly making a difference. I'd give my right arm to find bin Laden. All of us would. It would change the tempo of this war against the terrorists."

Nike understood army hunter-killer teams were all about finding terrorists and Taliban. "So, how are you feeling about this more peaceful assignment of working in this village as an ambassador of good will?"

"I like it."

"But it takes you off the front lines."

"Not really." Gavin looked to the north of the village. Kerosene lamps were lit and the mud and stone homes that had windows glowed golden. He liked dusk, even though from a wartime perspective, it was a killing time, when the enemy sneaked up and took lives. "With General Chapman coming here to Afghanistan, the priority has shifted to focus on these boundary villages. If we can get these people to trust us, they will let us know when Taliban are coming through. The villagers could be our eyes and ears. If we can stop the Taliban's advancement into this country, that's a good thing for everyone. In the end, it will save a lot of lives."

"I like your general's philosophy."

"So do I. If I could, I'd have world peace. As it is, there's world war."

Nike shook her head. "I grew up in a peaceful Greece."

"And yet, Greece has had its fair share of revolutions, too."

"Granted." Nike observed the pinkish sky, now fading. Darkness began to encroach across the narrow valley. "I wish for the day when there are no more wars anywhere. No more killing. I've seen enough of it. All people want to do is live in peace and get on with their lives."

"It's the same here," Gavin acknowledged. "Abbas was

saying that all he wanted for his people was to be left alone to eke out their survival in this valley. He's grown old before his time because of the Russians and now the Taliban intrusion."

"Afghanistan needs decades of peaceful downtime," Nike agreed. But there had been none for them.

A wonderful sense of happiness bubbled up within her but it warred with sadness at her loss of Antonio. Suddenly bothered by her proximity to Gavin, she frowned. "I don't know what's going on between us," she admitted quietly.

Gavin gazed down at Nike. Even in the semidarkness he could see the worry register in her face. "Why try to decipher it? Why not just let it be natural and flow?"

Her stomach was filled with those butterflies. The only other man to make her feel this way had been Antonio. "It's not that simple," she told him.

"When I first saw you, I thought you were the most beautiful woman I'd ever seen. Most of all, I liked your gold eyes," Gavin confided softly. "You have the look of a lioness."

Her heart beat a little harder. Gavin was sincere. Or at least, he sounded sincere. That meant she had to take his compliment seriously. Antonio had been so much like him: a gentle warrior, a man of philosophy, of much greater depth and breadth than most men. "Thank you. My grandmother had the same color eyes. They run in the women of our family."

"You're feeling tense. Why?"

Nike pulled out of his arms and faced him. Oh, she didn't want to do that, but if she remained in the protection of Gavin's arms, she would lose all reason. Did this man realize the mesmerizing power he had over her? She searched his hooded blue eyes. The shadows of the night made his face dark and fierce-looking. "Look, I've got a lot of past history, Gavin, and I don't want you to think the wrong things about us."

Hearing the desperation in her tone, he nodded. "What happened to make you feel this way?"

It was the right question. Again, Nike squirmed inwardly. She'd talked to no one about the loss of her beloved Antonio nearly two years ago. Only Dallas, who had been executive officer of BJS in Peru, knew the full story. She had been her confidante, her healer up to a point. A heaviness settled into Nike's chest and once more she felt old grief discharging from her wound. Opening her gloved hands, Nike said, "I fell in love with a Peruvian army officer whose job it was to locate and capture drug-runners." The next words were so hard to say, but Nike felt driven to give Gavin the truth. "Antonio was an incredible person. He had graduated from Lima's university in archaeology, but the men in his family all had served in the army. So he went in and I met him when he was a captain. He loved his country and he saw what the drug-running was doing to it. Without fail, he would volunteer for the most dangerous missions to eradicate the dealers."

"He sounds like a fine man," Gavin said. "Courageous."

"Yes, well, that courage got him killed," Nike bit out. Looking down at the dark, muddy ground, she added, "I told him that he was going to get killed if he kept it up. But he wouldn't listen. And then…it happened. Two years ago."

Gavin measured the look in her wounded eyes and heard the hurt in her husky voice. Reaching out, he placed his hand gently upon her drooping shoulders and whispered,

"I'm sorry. He must have been one hell of a man to get your attention."

Tiny ripples of heat radiated from where his hand had momentarily rested on her shoulder. Looking up, Nike searched Gavin's narrowed, intense blue eyes and shook her head. "Listen, I learned the hard way—in our business if you fall in love with a military person, you're going to lose him."

"That's not always true."

"Yes, it is."

Gavin heard the stubbornness in her tone. Looking into Nike's eyes for some hint that it wasn't the truth she really believed, he felt a sinking sensation in his gut. Something hopeful and newly born shattered in his chest. After all, he had been burned but good by Laurie Braverman a year ago. Gavin had sworn off military women for another reason. He hadn't lost someone he loved to death. He had lost her because they simply could not compromise with one another.

"Maybe you just need time," Gavin counseled gently, removing his hand. He ached to kiss Nike. The set of her full lips, the way the corners of her mouth were drawn in, told him the pain she still carried over the death of the Peruvian captain.

"No," Nike said grimly, "time isn't going to change my mind." She stared up at him, her voice firm. "You need to know the truth. I shouldn't have led you on. I'm sorry."

"I'm not sorry at all, Nike. Look, we all need someone at some time."

His mouth was so beautifully sculpted. Good thing he couldn't read her mind. He had the lips of Apollo, the sun god. And wasn't Gavin a bit of sunshine in her life? Nike didn't want to admit that at all. But he was. All day, she'd longed to have a few quiet, uninterrupted moments with him. She was hungry to find out who he was, his depth and what mattered to him. Far more curious than she should be, Nike said, "I can't need any man who is in the military, Gavin. Never again."

Looking toward the village that was barely outlined by the dying light, the windows gleaming with a golden glow, Nike sighed. "You deserve to know the truth."

"And I'm glad you trusted me with it." Gavin smiled down at her upturned face. Her lips parted and almost pleaded to be touched by his mouth. "It's a good first step, don't you think?"

Seeing that gleam in his eyes, Nike knew Gavin wanted to kiss her. Yet, he hadn't made a move. The tension swirled between them and her heart screamed for his kiss. Her past resurfaced, frightening her. If she surrendered to her desire for Gavin, she would be right back where she was before—heartbroken. "There are no other steps," she warned him.

"I don't believe that," Gavin said, his voice a low growl. Reaching out, he took that step forward, his arms coming around her shoulders. Surprise flared in her golden eyes, her need of him very readable and yet, as he closed the distance, Gavin could see her fear. As he gently brought Nike against him he wondered if she would resist. If she did, he'd instantly release her, of course. Gavin didn't want that to happen and he sensed she wanted him, too. He leaned down, searching, finding her parted lips.

The world exploded within Nike as her arms swept across his shoulders, his mouth capturing hers. It was a powerful kiss, yet gentle and welcoming. His lips were tentative and asking her to participate fully in the joy of connection. The moisture of his ragged breath flowed across her face. The whiskers of his beard were soft. Gavin's mouth guided her and slid wetly across her opening lips. He cajoled, passing his tongue delicately across her lower lip. Instantly, Nike inhaled sharply as the throbbing sensation dove deeply down between her thighs.

He smelled of sweat, of wool and the sharp, clean mountain air. She reveled in his weather-hardened flesh against her cheek. His arms were cherishing and Nike surrendered as he swept her hard against his body. Their breaths mingled as they explored one another like hungry, greedy beggars. Well, wasn't she? It had been two long years since she'd kissed a man. And how different Gavin's kiss was! Nike tried not to compare him to Antonio. Gavin's mouth wreaked fire from within her as his lips molded hotly with hers. One hand moved sinuously down the back of her jacket, following the curve of her back. His other hand held her close. Her nipples hardened instantly as he deepened their kiss.

Nike was starved! Her entire body trembled just as he reluctantly withdrew his mouth from her wet lips. Nike saw the glint of a hungry predator in his eyes as surely as it was mirrored in hers. Knees like Jell-O, Nike felt weak. Inwardly, her body glowed brightly and she yearned to know his touch upon her aching breasts, and how he would feel entering her.

All of these crazy sensations exploded through her now that they stood, watching each other in wonder. The night air was cold and their breath was like white clouds between them. Nike noted the satisfaction glittering in Gavin's narrowed eyes. He held her gently and didn't try to kiss her again.

"Now," Gavin rasped, "let's start all over. I'm me and you are you. I'm not the man from your past. I'm the one standing with you here in the present. Judging from the kiss,

I think we have something to build upon. I'm a patient man, Nike. I wasn't looking for a woman, but you walked into my life." His hand against the small of her back tightened. "And I'm not about to let you walk out of my life."

Chapter 5

Nike hadn't slept well and was finishing up breakfast with Jameela and her three daughters. Chapatis, a thin pita bread, had been filled with vegetables and seasoned with curry. She had trouble focusing on food when she kept remembering Gavin's kiss. It was completely unexpected—but welcome. Groaning inwardly, Nike remembered all her nightmares of Antonio's death. He'd been shot to death in the jungles of Peru. She'd sworn *never* to fall in love with a military man again. Not *ever*.

So why had she kissed Gavin? Why did she still want him? Nike had seen the predatory look in his eyes. She could have easily brushed him off. Why didn't she? *First things first: stop thinking about it.* Nike watched as the older daughters of the family cleared away the dishes and went to clean them in the kitchen.

Jameela was helping six-year-old Atefa wrap her leg, which had never had any surgical intervention. The little girl's leg was missing below the knee. Jameela had her daughter lie on the rug as she carefully wrapped the red, angry-looking stump with soft cotton fabric. Once it was tied in place, Atefa sat up and took her handmade crutches.

"Have you sought help for your daughter's missing leg?" Nike asked the mother.

"When it happened, we were shocked. My husband tried to get help from our government. He pleaded and begged a regional official to bring a doctor out here to help her," Jameela responded.

Nike frowned. "I'm so sorry. Who planted those mines?"

With a grimace, Jameela whispered, "The Afghan army did, to stop the Taliban."

Surprised, Nike blurted, "Why?"

"They hid them along the edges of our fields where we plow. They didn't want Talibans coming in here."

The whole conflict and mind-set of the Taliban didn't make sense. As soldiers, they could only do their part and hope families would be saved. Nike had to get to work pronto. Getting up, she shrugged on her coat and put the red scarf in place around her head. It was 0700 and dawn crawled up on the horizon. A mechanic team would arrive this morning to try and assess what was wrong with her CH-47. Every minute on the ground kept the helo a target of the Taliban. She had to get out and relieve her load master so he could come to Abbas's house and get breakfast.

"I'll come back later," Nike promised the woman. "Right now, I have to check my helicopter and relieve my sergeant."

Jameela stood and nodded. "Of course."

In the freezing cold of the spring morning, Nike hurried down the muddy, rutted street. The men were already busy.

A donkey hauled a wooden cart filled with wood brought from the slopes of the nearby mountains. She saw no one from Gavin's team, which was just as well. Right now, Nike couldn't bear to see him. She was too confused about what happened between them, that part of her wanted it to happen again…

Andy was delighted to see her and climbed out of the CH-47. He rubbed his gloved hands to warm them up. Even though Nike had provided heavy bedding for him, she knew it was no fun to sleep in a helo in freezing weather. After motioning for him to hightail it to the awakening village for breakfast, Nike took over watch of the helicopter. He handed her the binoculars.

Around her, the valley awakened. The brownish-red haze above the village came from the many wood fires prodded to life to feed a family in each of the mud-brick and stone dwellings. Above, the sky was a pale blue and she could see the tips of the mountains illuminated as the sun peeked above them. When the first rays slanted over the narrow valley, Nike could feel the warmth caressing her.

Dogs barked off and on. It seemed as if everyone had a dog or two. She never saw any cats and wondered why. Her breath was white as she exhaled. This was a very cold place even in the spring. But then, they were at eight thousand feet, so what did she expect? Moving around the helicopter, which sat out on a flat, muddy area, Nike looked for movement below. There didn't seem to be any, but she didn't trust the naked eye. The binoculars around her neck were a better way to search for the enemy.

Standing behind the helo for protection against sniping, she scanned the slopes below her. Nike noted small herds of sheep and goats being prodded out of the village center and down to the green grass below. It was a tranquil scene.

The sun's emergence had already upped the temperature by several degrees. Several dogs herded the animals farther down into the flat of the valley floor. It all looked so peaceful.

By the time Andy had gotten back to resume his duties, Nike was more than eager to go back to Jameela's home and grab another hot cup of the delicious and spicy chai tea. The woman had shared her secret recipe with Nike. Chai was individual to every family and Jameela's was legendary among the villagers. With some gentle persuasion, Nike got Jameela to divulge her recipe. Chai consisted of strongly boiled tea with goat milk, a pinch of brown sugar, cardamom and nutmeg. Her mouth watered just thinking about it.

She gave Andy a welcoming smile. He grinned as he walked up to her.

"Nothing?" he asked.

"No." Nike handed him the binoculars. "Keep watch. Captain Jackson was saying that the Taliban come through the northern end of this valley at the new moon, which is next week."

"Under cover of darkness," Andy said, placing the binoculars around his neck.

"Most likely, but you never know."

"I wouldn't know a Taliban from a villager. They all dress alike."

Grimly Nike said, "The villagers know they cannot approach this helo. So, if someone does, you draw your pistol and assume it's the enemy."

"Yes, ma'am. I just hope no one approaches," Andy said unhappily.

"I'll ask one of Captain Jackson's men to relieve you once an hour," Nike responded with understanding.

"Thanks." Andy looked up at the helo. "I'll sure be glad

to get out of here and back to base. I didn't sleep hardly at all last night."

"Neither did I." Nike smiled a little. Looking at her watch she said, "The team's supposed to arrive at 0800. That's not long from now."

"Can't be too soon. I'm spoiled," Andy said with a grin. "What I'd give for some bacon and eggs now. Not that the hot grain cereal wasn't good. It was."

Chuckling, Nike lifted her hand and walked back toward the village. Her heart thumped hard when suddenly she saw Gavin walking down the street, his rifle over his shoulder, looking as though he was hunting for someone. When he noticed her, his mouth lifted in a smile. He was the last person Nike wanted to see, but she couldn't turn around and avoid him.

"Good morning," Gavin called, catching the wariness in Nike's narrowed gold eyes. Those lips he'd caressed yesterday were pursed with tension. Over their kiss? He wasn't sure. Maybe she was upset over something else?

They met near the last mud-brick home. Both were aware that they might become targets and stepped into the alleyway between two homes for more protection. "I had sweet dreams," he told her.

"I didn't."

The flatness of her voice startled him. "Sorry to hear that. Everything okay?" He hooked a thumb toward her helo. Maybe Nike was discouraged over the fact her bird was down.

Nothing was okay, but she couldn't stand here discussing her personal stuff. Instead, she said, "You've seen Atefa? Abbas and Jameela's little girl who lost a leg to a land mine?"

"Yes."

"What are the chances of flying her and her mother out to Kabul to get some medical help with a prosthesis?"

Shrugging, Gavin said, "I could make some calls and find out."

"I'd appreciate that. That kid lost her leg to a land mine. She needs some type of medical help. Why can't the U.S. supply her with a prosthetic limb?"

Assuming Nike's worries were over the little girl, Gavin relaxed. Several black curls peeked out the sides of the red scarf she wore around her head. Nike looked even more vibrant and breathtaking to him. "There's no reason we can't. I've already radioed Kabul to tell them to get a medical doctor out here in the next two weeks."

"What about dental? A *lot* of people here have tooth problems," Nike said. She was relieved to be talking business with Gavin.

"Good idea. I hadn't gone that far with my plans for this village. Usually, it takes us a good three to four days to assess their health needs. Then I create a report and suggest a plan of action. After that, other medical or health teams are flown in to supplement the initial work we're doing right now."

"I see." Nike wasn't familiar with the tactics, but it sounded like a logical approach. "I think if you can help Atefa that it will go a long way to lessen Abbas's distrust toward us."

"Yeah, the old codger is definitely questioning everything we're doing," Gavin agreed quietly. "I'll give a call this morning to the medical people in Kabul. Several American programs help children who have lost limbs to land mines."

Warming to his concern, Nike tried not to look at his mouth. Memory of the kiss came back hot and sweet.

Frowning, she said abruptly, "Look, what happened yesterday is in the past, Gavin. I don't have time for any type of a relationship right now."

Gavin heard the desperation in her husky tone and trod carefully. "It was a shock for me, too," he admitted. "I came out of a relationship with a woman helicopter pilot about a year ago. I swore off military women." He gave her an uneven grin. "Until you came along."

Nike held up her hands. "Listen, I'm stopping this before it starts. I do *not* have room in my life." His blue eyes became assessing and furrows gathered on his brow. He took the Afghan cap off, pushed fingers through his short, dark hair and settled the cap back down on his head.

"It's not that easy, Nike. You know that."

"It is that easy." Feeling frantic, she couldn't face the stubborn glint in his eyes. "One kiss doesn't give you access to me or my life."

"That's true," he murmured. Gavin knew if he could just bring her back into his arms, capture her mouth, he'd persuade her differently. That time would come. But now, she was too scared, too prone to push him away. He had to let her go…a little bit. "I'm a patient person. Let's just take this a day at a time?"

"No." Giving him a hard look, Nike said, "It's *over,* Gavin. I'm sorry but I am not going to lose someone I love to a bullet. My heart just can't handle it. Do you understand?"

"Yes, I do," he answered honestly, feeling bereft. In his heart he knew that whatever they had would be long-term. Looking into Nike's eyes, however, he saw the fear and grief entwined. There was nothing he could do. Time to give up. "Wrong time and place."

"Exactly." Taking a step back, Nike said, "You're a nice

guy, Gavin. Maybe if we'd met a few years earlier… Oh, who knows? Just be safe, okay?"

As he watched Nike walk away, Gavin scowled. It felt as if someone had grabbed his heart and torn it out of his chest. Rubbing that sensitive area, he wondered how this beautiful Greek woman had captured him so easily. Gavin decided it was her personality. Nike had compassion for others, which his ex had lacked. Laurie had been out for herself and to hell with the rest of the world. By contrast, Gavin had seen Nike's care for others, whether it was concern for her load master, the people of this village or even his team.

"Well, hell," he muttered. Stepping out from between the homes, Gavin thought of the long day ahead. He was especially edgy because, according to headquarters, tonight was when the Taliban would start coming through the valley, and his mission would be to stop them dead in their tracks. Had the Taliban heard of their landing here, and were they coming in early instead? Ten men against a hundred of the enemy was not good odds. Gavin would not make the village a target. No, his team would take the fight with the Taliban elsewhere. He was glad of one thing: Nike would be out of here and safe. Her helo would be fixed and she'd be gone. That was important to Gavin.

Nike wanted to whoop for joy. She was sitting in the right-hand seat, her CH-47 idling along, both engines working once more. The mechanic team had arrived via Chinook and by noon, the damage to the front turbine was fixed. Andy, who was sitting in the copilot's seat, grinned like an idiot, but she understood why.

With her helmet on, she spoke into the microphone set close to her lips. "Okay, we're good to go. Did you contact Captain Jackson and let him know we were taking off?"

"Yes, ma'am, I did. He said for you to have a safe trip back to base."

Relieved, Nike gave him a thumbs-up. To her right, the first Chinook was taking off. Above them, an Apache circled to ensure no enemy was close to the U.S. Army helicopters. It felt good to have that firepower and she could hardly wait to get back to civilization. Andy left the seat and walked to the rear. Once she took the helo skyward, the ramp would be lowered and he'd be sitting out on the hip with the machine gun, watching for possible Taliban attacks from below.

Even though the helo shook and shuddered around her, Nike loved the sensations. Strapping in and tightening her harness, she radioed to the other helos. Within a minute, the rotors were at takeoff speed. Just feeling the Chinook unstick from the surface made Nike feel good. She saw a number of women and children at the village's edge watching in wonder. It was impossible to lift a hand and wave goodbye to them. One of her hands was on the cyclic, the other on the collective. Together, these kept the helicopter in stable, forward movement.

Most of all, Nike was relieved to leave Gavin behind. She felt guilty, but pushed all that aside. As the helo moved out over the green, narrow valley below, she followed the other Chinook at a safe distance. Within a minute, they'd begin their nap-of-the-earth flying, one hundred feet over the terrain in order to avoid being brought down by their enemy. Pursing her lips, Nike focused on the business at hand. For at least an hour, she wouldn't have to think about Gavin. Or about his kiss that had rocked her world.

"Any word from that A team in Zor Barawul?" Nike asked the communications tech in the ops building. It was nearly midnight and Nike couldn't sleep. She was worried about Gavin and his team interdicting the Taliban in the valley.

The woman shook her head. "Nothing—yet."

"Okay, thanks," Nike muttered. She shoved her hands into the pockets of her trousers and walked out of the small building. Above, the stars twinkled brightly, looking so close Nike could almost reach out and touch them. There wasn't much light around the camp, which helped keep it hidden from the enemy. She had a small flashlight and used it to get to her tent.

Just being back on the roster and assigned an Apache helicopter made Nike feel better. At least she was off the workhorse helicopter list. Despite this, worry tinged her happiness. Five minutes didn't go by without her thinking of Gavin or remembering the heated kiss they'd shared.

"Dammit," she breathed softly. Why, oh why couldn't she just let that kiss go? Stop remembering the strength of his arms around her? The pressure of his mouth caressing her lips as if she were some priceless object to be cherished?

Upon reaching her tent, she pulled the flap aside and then closed it. The warmth from the electric heater made all the difference in the world. Each of the twenty women Apache pilots got a small tent with a heater and a ply-board floor. The cot wasn't much, but it was a helluva lot better than what she'd had at the village.

Because she was on duty for the next twenty-four hours, Nike remained in her clothes. She took off her armor and boots and laid them at the foot of her cot. She had to sleep, but how? She worried about Gavin and his team. Had they discovered the Taliban coming across the valley yet? Lying down, she brought her arm across her eyes. And then, in minutes, she fell asleep—a small blessing.

Chapter 6

"This week, you're assigned to the CH-47," Emma Trayhern-Cantrell, the XO, told Nike as they sat together at an ops table. "You're going to be bringing in supplies to several boundary villages. And we're short on copilots, so you're flying without one."

Thanks," she told her XO. Nike nodded and tried to hide her disappointment. For a week, she'd flown the aggressive Apache and done her fair share of firing off rockets and rounds to protect A teams up in the mountains hunting Taliban. Because she loved the adrenaline rush, it was tough to be relegated to a lumbering workhorse instead.

Her XO handed her the list of villages along with the supplies to go to them and the times of delivery. Emma Trayhern was all business. She had the red hair of a Valkyrie with large gray eyes and a soft mouth. She had her uncle Morgan Trayhern's eyes. However, Nike already knew that this Trayhern child was no pushover even if her face spoke of openness and compassion. Emma was an Apache pilot and as tough as they came.

"I know you're bummed. CH's don't rock." Emma tried to smile. "There's always dirty work along with the rockin' Apache. You're just lucky enough to have skills in the CH-47."

"Yeah," Nike said grumpily, folding up the orders. "I wish they'd give us another Apache or two."

Shaking her head, Emma said, "They're stretched to the max over in Iraq. We get the leftovers. It sucks, but it is what it is."

"I'm not so philosophical," Nike said, rising. It was near dawn, a red ribbon on the eastern horizon outside the ops hut. Already, the air base was in full swing and with plenty of action.

"You hear anything about your guy? Captain Jackson?"

Giving Emma a frown, Nike said, "He's *not* my guy. How did that rumor get started?"

Grinning, Emma folded up the huge map and left it on the ops table. "Blame your load master, Andy."

"Blabbermouth," Nike muttered.

"We were expecting the Taliban to go down through that valley near Zor Barawul, but they didn't. I told Dallas that I thought someone from the village probably sneaked off to tell them the A team was in town, so they took another trail into the country."

"I wouldn't doubt it," Nike said. She put the paper into the thigh pocket of her dark green flight suit. "When I was there overnight, there was a lot of wariness toward Americans."

"Well," Emma said, "you'll be delivering the last load of the day to them. If you get a chance, stay on the ground for an hour and find out what's going on. I like to get eyes and ears out there on those villages. Dallas wants to keep a check on them and whether they get slammed by the Taliban."

"Good idea." Nike wasn't too sure she wanted to spend an hour on the ground to visit with Gavin. She saw the curiosity in Emma's eyes. "I'll do my best."

"Do it at each stop, Nike. We want you to talk to the leader of each team and get their latest assessment."

It wasn't a bad idea, Nike thought as she put on her black BJS baseball cap. "Okay, will do," she promised. "This is going to be more like a milk run."

Emma walked her to the door. "I hope you're right. But be careful. Those four villages are not on our side. Yet."

"Getting food, medical personnel and medicine in to them on a regular basis will help," Nike said, opening the door. The crisp air was barely above freezing. Nike would be glad when June came. Everyone said it got warmer at the beginning of that month. In the mountains at eight thousand feet, a local gardener told her that there was less than a ninety-day growing period. This made gardening tough, which was why most people had goats, chickens, sheep and few vegetables. Certainly, fruit was scarce, too.

Clapping her on the shoulder, Emma reminded her, "Be careful out there. Dallas does *not* want to lose any of her pilots."

Grinning, Nike gave her a mock salute and said, "Oh, not to worry, XO. We're a tough bunch of women." She decided to swing by the base exchange and picked up four boxes of dates and four pounds of candy for the kids. Dates were a delicacy usually eaten only at the time of Ramadan. Poor villages couldn't afford such a wonderful fruit and Nike wanted to give it to the wife of the chief of each village. The meaning of her exchange would go far with the women of the village to cement a positive connection. And the children would love the sweets. That made her smile because the Afghan children were beautiful, so full of life and laughter.

Gavin was surprised as hell to see Nike walking toward him from the helicopter. She'd covered her short, shining dark curls with a black baseball cap. He grinned, feeling his heart open up.

"Hey," he called, "this is a pleasant surprise."

Her lips tingled in anticipation. Nike could see the happiness burning in his blue eyes as he approached her. While part of her wanted to rush into Gavin's arms, she halted a good six feet from him, hands on her hips. "Just dropping off supplies, a doctor and dentist, and getting the lay of the land and giving Jameela a box of dates as a goodwill gesture."

Gavin sensed her unease but kept his smile. "Dates. That's a great idea." He added, "I missed you."

Though wildly flattered, Nike couldn't get on a personal footing with him. Lucky for them, there was all kinds of activity around the unloading of the helo. A number of men carried the cardboard boxes into the village. The doctor and dentist were led into a group of awaiting men and boys. "My boss wants me to spend an hour with you getting a sense of how things are going at the village. She's compiling an ongoing dialogue with the generals above her on where each village stands."

Raising his brows, Gavin said, "You ladies are on top of things." He gestured for her to follow him. "Come on, we'll go to the team house, have some chai and chat."

Nike did not want to be alone with Gavin. He was too

damned masculine. She wished for the thousandth time her traitorous body would stop clamoring for another kiss from him. Her mind was in charge and no way could she get involved again. Ever. "Okay, but this is business, Captain."

"No problem," Gavin said smoothly.

Walking at his shoulder, a good twelve inches between them, Nike said, "You never got that attack you were expecting. I'm glad."

Gavin dodged the muddy ruts made by the continuous donkey-cart traffic through the village. "Yeah, we're relieved. But suspicious." The sun had warmed the village and children played in the late afternoon. Dogs ran around barking and chasing one another. Women in burkas were here and there, but mostly, they moved the window curtains aside to stare at them walking by.

Nike saw a number of barefoot children with mud up to their knees. She smiled a little. They were tough little kids in her opinion and yet, so huggable. She started handing out the bag of candy she carried in her hand. In no time, every child in the village surrounded them. Nike made sure each child, no matter how little, got a handful of jellybeans. When it was gone, they disappeared with their treasures. She turned to Gavin. "I'm glad for you it's been quiet around here. Why do you think that happened?"

Gavin nodded as they sauntered toward the stone home on the left. "We think the Taliban got tipped off by someone here in the village and they decided to take other paths into the country."

"But that doesn't guarantee anything for long," Nike said.

"True, but we're making progress. Abbas is softening his stance toward us. He's still worried the Taliban will see him consorting with us. And I think someone in the village was scared to death of the same thing, intercepted the Taliban and told them to take another track. That way, it would look like this village was still helping the Taliban. It's a real balancing act out here for Abbas." Gavin halted and gestured to a large mud-brick home. "Here we are. Come on in. I'm ready for some hot chai."

Inside, the hard-packed earth had been swept. Everything was clean and neat. The men's equipment stood up against the walls in neat rows. There was a stove in the corner with plenty of wood, the tin chimney rising up and out of the roof. The windows were clean and sunlight made the room almost bright, if not cheerful.

"Have a seat," Gavin said, taking off his hat and putting his rifle nearby. He shrugged out of the dark brown tunic and then removed his body armor. "Feels good to get out of this thing," he muttered. "I live in it almost twenty-four hours a day."

"Armor is the pits," Nike agreed. She saw several small rugs and pillows near the stove. Taking a seat on one, she watched as Gavin went through the motions of putting water in a copper kettle and then sitting it on top of the stove. Her heart pined for his arms around her, his mouth cherishing her lips. For now, she fought her desire, crossed her legs and folded her hands in her lap.

"If your CO wants to know about this village," Gavin said, pulling a tin of loose tea off a shelf, "tell her that we've got about a twenty-percent pro-American base here now. The men are starting to open up to us."

"Is that all?" Nike pulled out a notebook and a pen from her left pocket.

Gavin filled the tea strainer and gave her a one-raised-eyebrow look. "Is that all? It's only been a week. I think that's pretty amazing."

Jotting it down, Nike said, "I've brought a medical doctor and a dentist and hygienist with me. That ought to encourage a little more loyalty."

He poured hot water into two tin mugs and then dipped in the strainer filled with loose tea. "If we could gain loyalty like that, all we'd have to do is hand out money and buy them off."

"I understand."

"Honey?"

"Yes, please." She watched as he poured goat's milk into the mixture and pulled another tin from the shelf. He ladled out a teaspoonful of golden honey into each cup. Another tin contained a spice mixture and he put a pinch into the steaming chai. There was something solid and steady about Gavin. He had a confidence born from experience in the field. Everything he did had a sureness to it. Nike realized that he was the kind of leader anyone could trust completely. That was just another reason to like him way too much.

Gavin brought over the steaming mug. "Chai for two," he teased. He set his cup on the ground and brought up a small gold rug and pillow, sitting opposite her. "And I know Jameela's chai rocks, but she isn't about to give her secret recipe to anyone." He chuckled.

"She gave it to me. I loved staying at her home. At the base I keep trying different chai mixtures to duplicate it, but so far, no luck." Nike sipped the delicious chai. "Hey, this isn't bad, Jackson." She tried to relax, but being so close to him made her squirm endlessly. Not to mention Gavin seemed even more handsome with his long-sleeved cotton shirt and brown Afghan trousers. His beard, as always, was meticulously shaped and trimmed. Even his hair was longer in order to emulate the Afghan men's hairstyle. His skin was so suntanned he could easily have passed for an Afghani.

"So, did you miss me?" he inquired with a wicked grin.

Nike refused to meet his eyes. Her hands tightened imperceptibly around the tin mug. "I didn't have time."

"Pity," Gavin teased. He saw how uncomfortable Nike had become. Yet, her cheeks reddened and there had to be a reason for it. "Well," he said conversationally, "I sure missed you."

"I wish you wouldn't."

"Why?"

"You know why, Gavin. I just can't fall for another military man."

"Oh, that's right—you think I'll die in combat."

"There's a damn good chance of that."

"Well," he pointed out, "look at you. You have an Apache strapped to your butt and you're always a fair target for the Taliban, too."

"That's different."

"How? A bullet is a bullet."

"You're infuriating. Were you on the debate team at your college?"

"Actually, a university. And yes, I was on the debate team for four years. I like arguing." He flashed a smile even when revealing this nugget of truth.

"Of course you do." Nike couldn't help but smile back, all while trying to steady her racing heart. "Which university?"

"Princeton. Where did you get your degree?"

"The University of Athens."

He gave her a warm look. "Congratulations."

There was an uncomfortable pause and Nike could feel him warming up for some heady declaration. Why couldn't this be a business meeting? Well, she knew why but just couldn't face it.

Sipping his chai, he sighed. "I've dreamed about you every night. About our kiss."

"That's your problem." Nike had to look away, until she realized she was being a coward.

"I don't believe you mean that." Gavin searched her narrowing gaze. "You're scared, Nike. That doesn't mean there isn't something between us. I grant this is a lousy place to become aware of it. I'm interested in you for all the right reasons. And I know why you're gun-shy. But can't you give us a chance?"

His words were spoken so softly that Nike felt her heart bursting with need of him. This was a side to him she'd not been aware of until now. "I'll bet you are a damned good used-car salesperson, too."

Laughing heartily, Gavin finished off his chai, got to his feet and made a second cup for himself. "Thank you for the compliment. Frankly, I'd rather sell you on me."

"I got that." She sipped her chai and wanted to run away. The room became smaller and smaller and Nike felt trapped. Or maybe she was trapping herself.

"My team is coming back in a week to base camp," he told her conversationally, sitting down once more. "We get two days off. I'd like to take you to Jalalabad, to a nice little restaurant I know about, and have dinner with you. How about it?"

"I don't think so, Gavin."

"Are you sure? I see some hesitation in your eyes."

Setting the cup down next to her knee, Nike said, "I just can't."

Nodding, Gavin said nothing. His instincts were powerful and he knew she liked him. Just how much, he didn't know. He'd tried to play fair and that hadn't worked. Honesty wasn't necessarily the best policy with Nike, who was jumpy and wary. While he understood her reasons, Gavin wasn't about to back down. He watched as she drew out her notebook and pen once more.

"Ready for my village assessment?" he asked her. Instantly, he saw Nike's face relax. So long as he remained on a professional, hands-off basis with her, she wasn't distrusting.

"More than ready." Nike looked at the watch on her wrist. "I have to lift off in thirty minutes."

"No problem." Gavin launched into the many details, names, events and places that he knew her CO would want. It was still an unadulterated pleasure to be with her. She was a feast for his eyes, balm for his heart and Gavin felt as if her presence pumped him full of life and hope again.

Nike just about ran out the door of the house when they were done. She did not want Gavin to trap and kiss her. If he ever kissed her again, she'd melt away in his arms, completely defenseless against his heated onslaught. Moving out into the late-afternoon sunshine, she saw that the shipment of boxes had been removed from the CH-47. Next, she visited Jameela at her home and gave her the box of dates. The woman nearly cried, threw her arms around Nike and hugged her.

"You are my sister," Jameela whispered, wiping her eyes as she held the precious box of dates.

Feeling the warmth of true friendship, Nike reached out

and squeezed her hand. "All women are sisters," she told her with a grin.

Jameela nodded and understood exactly what Nike was saying. In this man's world, ruled by men and where women were considered secondhand in every way, they needed to band together and support one another. "The next time you visit, you must have time to have chai with me," Jameela said.

"Ah, I love your chai," Nike said with a laugh. "And yes, if I get this mission again, I'll ask my CO for a half hour more and we'll sit and talk over chai."

Bowing her head, Jameela's eyes burned with warmth. "I would like that, my sister. Allah keep you safe."

"Thank you," Nike murmured, meaning it sincerely. "I can use all prayers." She left the house and hurried down the muddy street. She wanted to do nothing more than get out of here and away from that man who drove her to distraction.

Nike ordered Andy into the helo to raise the ramp, and she settled into her right-hand seat. Just the act of putting on her helmet and running through the flight list before takeoff soothed her taut nerves. From time to time, Nike would give a quick glance out the window, looking for Gavin to show up. He had a way of quietly walking up to her so that she never heard him coming. Not today.

Within minutes, they were airborne. Some small part of her was disappointed that Gavin hadn't come to see her lift off. Moving the heavy two-engine helo into the blue sky, Nike now had to focus on more important things—like surviving this flight back to base.

As she flew nap-of-the-earth throughout the region, she never took the same route twice. Consequently, the route through the mountains was always different and filled with unexpected new difficulties. Nike was glad for the challenge. It kept her mind—and her heart—off Gavin. Still, even as she flew, she wondered what would happen when he and his team came back to base for a two-day rest.

Chapter 7

Nike was halfway back to base when she got orders to turn around and head back to Zor Barawul. Stymied by the clipped radio message, she had no choice but to do so.

As she landed near dusk, the sun tipping the western mountains, she saw Gavin standing with Jameela and her daughter, Atefa. The whirling blades of her helicopter kicked up heavy clouds of dust.

By the time she got out of her harness and placed her helmet on the seat, Gavin was at the rear of the ramp.

"What's going on?" she asked.

"The medical doctor just approved Atefa to be flown to Kabul to be fitted for a prosthesis." He grinned. "I called your base and asked that you return. Sorry to do this. I know it's damn dangerous flying in and out of here."

"Don't worry about it," Nike said, looking out the ramp door at Jameela, who stood with a protective arm around her young daughter. "Is Abbas in favor of this?"

"He is. That's the best news." He searched her face. "I've already talked to the CO of the base. We need to fly them in now and preparations are under way to give them a tent and food for the night. Tomorrow morning, the three of us will be flown to Kabul."

"You're coming along?" Her heart beat once to underscore that news.

"Yes. I'm leaving Sergeant Bailey in charge while I'm gone."

"But…"

"The threat of attack here is always high," Gavin said, reading her concern. "I've gotten permission from my superior to do this because they feel this particular village is essential in the fight against the Taliban."

"And Jameela and Abbas trust you." Nike nodded. "It makes sense." She managed a slight smile. "Have you warned them about the rough ride and nap-of-the-earth flying we'll be doing?"

"I have. What I want to do is get Jameela and her daughter strapped in behind you and I'll ride shotgun in the copilot seat if that's all right with you?"

Her smile turned devilish. "Sounds good to me. If I get shot you can take over flying."

Gavin recognized her black humor and chuckled. "Right. I have a pair of gold-plated tin wings from a United flight attendant that makes me pilot material. Will that do?"

"You're a piece of work, Jackson."

"But you like me anyway, right?"

Seeing the glimmer of warmth in his eyes, Nike waved a hand at him and walked down the ramp. "There's no way I'm answering that one." She gestured for the pair to come forward. After giving Andy orders, she walked back into the bird. Gavin had passed her on the ramp, walking down to meet the twosome. Nike noticed most of the village had turned out to watch. She had to remind herself that these people, cut off from the outside world, hadn't seen helicopters since the Russians tried to ransack their country decades earlier. The CH-47 was a curiosity among them, especially the younger children.

Jameela walked slowly and kept a hand on her curious daughter as they boarded the helicopter. Nike finished off her radio message to her base and then turned around. Lifting her hand, she waved hello to Jameela, who was draped in her black burka. Nike could only see her wider-than-usual eyes. The woman must not ever have flown in any type of aircraft. Feeling for her, Nike went back, knowing that a smile might make the woman feel more at ease.

As Jameela grabbed her hand, Nike said, "It's okay, Jameela. Everything will be all right." She leaned over and gave Atefa a hug. The little girl was dressed in her finest, most colorful robe, her black hair brushed to perfection. Atefa's eyes shone with excitement.

Jameela gave the ramp door a desperate look and still gripped Nike's hand.

"She's scared to death," Nike said to Gavin, who had come up behind her.

"I know. Show her to the nylon seat behind your seat. I'm sure being near another woman will help calm her fears."

Nike didn't disagree. She took Jameela to the nylon webbed seat and asked her to sit. The woman did, with great reluctance. Nike had to guide her carefully to the seat so she wouldn't trip and fall over her burka.

After getting the harness in place around Jameela, Nike attended to Atefa in the next seat. Andy took the girl's crutches and tied them down next to their two stacked suitcases strapped down on the deck of the helo. Atefa's eyes were huge as she scanned the cargo hold of the helicopter. Nike kept smiling and murmuring words of encouragement as she ensured they were strapped in.

Next came the helmets. They had none that would fit Atefa, so Andy brought over a pair of earphones and clapped them over her head so she would have protection from the horrendous sounds within the airborne helo. Jameela pulled on hers and was hooked up to the communications system. This way Gavin could continue to answer her questions and soothe her throughout the flight.

In minutes, the ramp groaned and squealed as it came up and closed. The cargo hold was thrown into semidarkness. Patting Jameela's shoulder, Nike went to her seat, pulled on her helmet and got ready to take the bird up.

Andy sat down next to the twosome and Gavin explained to Jameela that he was there to support her through the flight. Jameela seemed less intimidated when Andy strapped himself in next to her. Nike's large, broad seat back on one side and the young man on the other seemed to calm her fears, Gavin thought.

After climbing into the copilot's seat, Gavin picked up the extra helmet and put it on, opening communication between the four of them. As she rapidly went through the preflight checklist, Nike's gloved hands flew across the instrument panel. She was focused on this flight, not on the man next to her. He must have understood the gravity of this dangerous flight and wasn't about to distract her. For that, she was grateful.

The flight back wasn't any different from any other, but Gavin had his hands full with Jameela, who screamed into the helmet's mouthpiece whenever they dived and wove through the mountain passes at a hundred feet. Nike couldn't afford to pull her focus off her flying. The CH-47 shook and shuddered like a dog shaking off fleas as she guided it up and down and then twisted around the mountains to plunge down into the next valley.

By the time they arrived at the base, Jameela was frantic. Atefa, however, was laughing and throwing her arms up and down. For the child, it was like a fun roller-coaster ride.

By custom, no man could touch the woman, so it was Nike who unharnessed Jameela and Atefa, taking off the helmet and earphones and walking them down the ramp into the dusk. Andy brought along the suitcases. A medic met them at the bottom of the ramp in a golf cart, ready to whisk them to a tent for the night.

By the time Nike had them settled, it was pitch-dark. Gavin met her outside the tent.

"They all set?"

"Yes. Finally." Nike quirked her mouth. "What a day."

Gavin nodded and fell into step with her as they headed to the chow hall on the other side of the base. "Couldn't have done it without you. Thanks. I know Jameela feels better because she knows you and trusts you." No lights marked the camp after night fell. To have it lit up was to invite attacks by the Taliban. Each of them had a small flashlight to show the way between the rows of green canvas tents.

The cool night air revived Nike. She was always tense after such a flight. It felt good to talk about little things, and, even though she didn't want to admit it, she was glad to have Gavin's company. After chow, she'd go to ops and fill out her mission debrief report.

Inside the large, plywood-floored tent, the odor of food permeated the air. Nike found herself hungry, so they went through the line and ended up at a wooden picnic table in the corner. She eagerly sipped her hot coffee. Gavin sat opposite her.

"You a little hungry?" she teased Gavin, who sat opposite her, digging into roast beef slathered with dark brown gravy.

"Listen, when you eat as many MREs as we do, real food is a gift," he said, popping a piece of beef into his mouth.

Nike could only imagine. There were mashed potatoes with that thick, brown gravy, corn with butter and a huge biscuit. She ate as if she'd never seen food. Normally, she didn't have such a large appetite, but tonight, she did. "This hits the spot," she told him.

"Mmm," Gavin mumbled, barely breathing between bites.

Nike grinned. "If you don't slow up, you're going to choke on that food you're shoveling down your gullet."

Chastised, Gavin had the good grace to flush. He slowed down a little. "You have no idea how good real, hot food tastes."

"I probably don't. I'm spoiled. I might fly every day or night, but I can come here and get good chow. I hate MREs."

"Everyone does," he said between bites. He took his third biscuit and pulled it open. After putting in several slabs of butter, he took a big bite.

Nike saw the absolute pleasure the food gave him. She knew these A teams were out in the wilds for a month at a time, sometimes more. This unexpected trip was a real present to Gavin. She tried to ignore how handsome he was, even with the full beard.

"Do you mind wearing your disguise?" she wondered, pushing her empty plate to one side. She held the white ceramic mug of coffee between her hands.

"No."

"It's got to be different from the spit and polish of shaving every day."

"Oh, that." Gavin touched his neatly trimmed beard. "I bet you wonder what I look like without it?"

"No…"

"Sure you do." He grinned.

"I was just wondering how you liked going under cover."

Shrugging, Gavin finished off his third and final biscuit. "Doesn't bother me. Usually, when we're out for a month, we're riding horses and doing our thing."

"So you've all learned how to ride."

"That or fall off." He laughed. Scraping up the last of the gravy, he sighed. "That was damn good food. I wish I could take this back to the guys."

"You and your team go without a lot of things," Nike said, feeling bad for them.

"Luck of the draw," Gavin said. He wiped his mouth with his paper napkin, pushed the plate aside and then picked up his cup of coffee. "I'd rather be on the ground than threading the needle with that hulking helo of yours. That must take some starch out of you."

"Sure it does. Seat-of-the-pants kind of flying. I don't mind doing nap-of-the-earth. I do mind getting shot at."

Chuckling, Gavin felt the warmth of the food in his belly. How lucky he was that Nike had shared such a meal with him. He felt happiness threading through him like sun shining into a dark valley. "Makes two of us. I felt for Jameela. The poor woman is probably going to refuse to step into the CH-47 tomorrow morning."

"We'll have to persuade her that the flight to Kabul will

be smooth and quiet, unlike the snaking flight from her village."

"I don't know if she'll believe me," Gavin said.

"She'll get on board because her daughter is going to be fitted for a new leg."

"I appreciate all you did. If you hadn't been there, this would have been a lot tougher. Moslem customs don't allow any man to touch a woman."

Shaking her head, Nike muttered, "I'm glad I was there, but I can't see how their women live in such a state. I know I couldn't."

"Different realities, different belief system," Gavin said. "We don't have to like it for ourselves, but we have to understand and respect them for it."

"Glad I'm a woman from a democracy, thank you very much."

Gavin smiled. "Dessert? I saw some great-looking cherry pie over there. Want some?"

"Sure."

He got up. "Ice cream on it?"

In that moment, Nike saw he was like a little boy in a candy store. The light dancing in his readable blue eyes made her heart melt. "Why not?"

"Be right back."

She watched him thread his way through the noisy, busy place. This was the dinner hour and the place was packed with crews. There were a few A teams, as well, all dressed in their Afghan clothing. Still, as she allowed her gaze to wander around the area, Nike thought Gavin Jackson stood head and shoulders above any other man present. Maybe she was prejudiced. Maybe she liked him more than she should.

Feeling uneasy for a moment, Nike didn't question why

she decided to have a meal with him. If she was really sincere about not ever wanting to love a military man again, she'd have left him at the chow hall and disappeared. But she hadn't. *Damn*. Rubbing her face, Nike felt torn. The problem was, Gavin was too easy to like.

His eyes were shining with triumph when he came back with two large plates. His had two pieces of cherry pie and scoops of vanilla ice cream. Setting hers down in front of her, he gloated, "I couldn't help myself. I love cherry pie and ice cream. My parents have a farm in Nebraska and I grew up picking sour cherries from our trees so Mom could make these mouthwatering pies."

"You're something else," Nike murmured. She watched him sit down and launch into the dessert without apology. Indeed, he was a little ten-year-old boy and not the man sitting there. His expression was wreathed with such pleasure that Nike couldn't help but laugh.

"So, you're a Nebraska farm boy?"

"Yep. My folks have a five-hundred-acre farm. They raise organic wheat, corn and soybeans for the growing green market. Of course, they were doing this decades earlier."

"And you helped with all the farming?"

"Me and my two younger brothers," Gavin said, shoveling in another bite of cherry pie. "They're still at the farm and will take it over when Dad decides to retire."

Cocking her head, she asked, "So, what made you come into the military, then?"

Shrugging, he wiped his mouth. "The excitement. I get bored real easy and watching corn grow wasn't exactly my kind of fodder."

"So, this is your career?"

"I plan to put twenty in, retire and then do a lot of things I couldn't do before."

"Like what?"

He gave her a wistful look. "I like to travel. I want to see the countries of the world, large and small. I enjoy meeting people of different beliefs and religions. I always learn from them and it makes me a better person in the end."

"I'd never have thought that of you."

"No?" Gavin asked, lifting his head and giving her a thoughtful look. "What did you think?"

Uncomfortable, Nike said, "I don't know. I just never thought that much about it." *Liar.*

"I see. Well, how about you? You're Greek by birth. How did you get into the U.S. Army to fly Apaches?"

The pride in his tone washed across Nike. Plenty of men distrusted her because she was a woman in the pilot's seat of an Apache. "My father was in the Greek military for twenty years and then went into flying for a commercial airline. I grew up wanting to fly. He made sure I had flight lessons on single-engine airplanes from the time I was fourteen years old. Later, I wanted to fly helicopters, so I got my license when I was seventeen. My mother didn't want me to go into the military, fearing I'd die."

Gavin nodded. "Not a prudent choice from her perspective."

"No, but I was a tumbleweed of sorts. I didn't want to do things girls were supposed to do. All I wanted to do was get in the sky. I loved the challenge of flying a helo versus a fixed-wing aircraft. When I was up in the sky, everything in my life went right."

"On the ground, things got muddied up?"

"You got it."

"Was there a program for flying the Apache?"

"There was, and I took advantage of it. After I graduated from school in the U.S., I was assigned to the Black Jaguar Squadron down in Peru. I spent several years chasing the druggies and loved every moment of it. From there, I got assigned to chasing druggies along the U.S.–Mexican border. Dallas, who was already there, got me assigned to her unit. When she told me the Pentagon was going to approve a second all-woman BJS squadron, I wanted to be a part of it."

"And here you are. That's pretty impressive."

"Thank you. Women can do anything they want if they dream high enough."

"Obviously, you're one hell of a dreamer."

She chuckled and relaxed completely. Talking to Gavin was like talking to her best friend. "I don't think everyone dreams of being in combat, though. I like the challenge of it. I don't like thinking about getting killed. No one does."

"So, what other dreams do you have?"

She took a sip of her coffee. "I'd like to go back to Apache school in the U.S. and teach. I think I'd be a good instructor."

"So, you dream of twenty years in the military, too?"

"I guess I do, but I'm focused only on the present. My mother is always urging me to get married, have kids and come back to live in Greece. I told her I was too young for all of that. I've seen people get married too early, get bogged down with children, and then they're forty-five before they ever have a life of their own. I love kids, and I want them, but not right now. I want to use my twenties and thirties to explore what moves me in life. After that, I'll settle down."

"Sounds like a plan," Gavin said before his expression

became serious. "You said the man you loved was killed in combat down in Peru?"

"Yes." Nike hesitated.

"I know what it's like to lose someone you care for. In my first deployment here in Afghanistan, I lost two of my men from my team."

"I'm sorry." And she was. Nike saw his straight, dark brows dip in grief. "I'm just now coming to terms with the loss of Antonio."

"I'm sure we'll both remember those we loved forever."

She liked his sensitivity. "Love can't be destroyed."

"I found that with their loss, I became overprotective and superconservative when I was out in the field. I didn't want to lose any more of my men."

"That's understandable."

"Well, it got to the point where my own men got frustrated with me. I was scared. So, I pulled back, and I lost my will to go out and be the risk-taker I was before. At the end of my first tour, my men finally had to sit me down and let me have it. They told me that risk is a part of our nature, that avoidance wasn't going to help them live or die. Eventually, I realized they were right," Gavin murmured. "I was afraid to connect with life again. My fear paralyzed me in a lot of ways I couldn't see then. I do now, but my men had to gang up on me and force me to see how I was reacting."

She saw the caring in Gavin's blue eyes as he held her gaze. "I can see why you became so gun-shy, so to speak. I hope you don't blame yourself for what happened."

"I try not to." Gavin sat up and moved his shoulders as if to get rid of accumulated tension. "It didn't want to take another chance and that kept me from my job, from living. My men saw it and came to my rescue."

"They are good friends to you, then."

"And I want to be a friend to you, Nike."

His words, softly spoken, made her heart hammer suddenly. Gazing into his eyes, Nike could feel him wanting to reach out and touch her hand. "A friend?" she asked stupidly.

"You're afraid to get back into life because you lost the man you loved. I know you want to protect yourself." Gavin smiled warmly, the expression making her ache inside. "But life isn't like that. You can't help who you do or don't fall in love with. It's chemistry and a million other things all rolled into one."

"Where is this going?" She tried not to look at him but it was impossible

"I'd like to be your friend, but you won't let me."

"You want a lot more, Gavin. I can't give that to you."

Sighing, he nodded. "I know. The problem is, I like you. I'd like to get to know you better on your time and terms. I'm not the kind of guy who hops from bed to bed. You're different from any woman I've ever met. You're courageous, you have steel nerves and you're intelligent. All those things draw me to you. I didn't plan this, it just happened."

His honesty made her feel guilty, especially since there was so much she liked about him. It had been a long time since someone had touched her on such a deep level. "Gavin, you're a nice guy, but I just can't."

Getting up, she left the chow hall as quickly as she could. Her heart was hurting and the grief still roiled within her. The cold night air gave her the slap in the face she needed. She felt bad that she had stomped all over Gavin for being honest. Nike didn't like herself very much as she made her way to her tent. Weaving through the tent city, she noticed the stars twinkling above. They were cold, distant and beautiful. If only she could feel that distant and cold toward Gavin.

Every time the guy looked at her, she found herself shaky, needy and sexually hungry. Was Gavin right? Was this all about her own fear of loss? Of course it was. Nike halted in front of her tent and shut off the flashlight. In the distance, she heard an Apache revving up to take off on a night mission. The wind was cold and she shivered. As she recalled Gavin's story about losing his men, she realized he was trying gently to tell her something about herself.

With a muffled curse, Nike turned, pulled open the flap on her tent and went inside. She sat on the cot and took off her flight boots. Tears burned in her eyes and she wiped them away almost instinctively. She was drawn to Gavin Jackson whether she wanted it or not! A sense of guilt and a need to run flooded her.

The worst part was Gavin had no unlikeable qualities. This fact compelled her to throw her boots across the floor. They made thunks as they struck the plywood. Leaning over, elbows on her thighs, Nike pressed her hands to her face. She wanted to keep crying. Of all things! It had been two years since she'd cried and that was at Antonio's funeral.

"Damn you, Jackson."

Chapter 8

The July heat was arid and scalding. Nike had grown up in the dry heat of her homeland, Greece, so she felt right at home. Red-haired Emma Trayhern-Cantrell and she trotted across the tarmac to their waiting Apache helicopter. The crew quickly opened up the canopies. Word had just come in that an A team near the village of Bar Sur Kamar was under heavy attack.

Time was of the essence. Nike was the AC, air commander. She leaped up on the step and quickly situated herself in the forward cockpit. Her heart pounded in time with the snaps her harness made as she fastened it. Emma climbed into the rear seat, behind Nike. A blonde mechanic by the name of Judy cinched them in and gave them a thumbs-up before removing the ladder and hauling it beyond the range of the helo's blades.

"Ready," Emma told Nike from the rear seat.

"Good to go," Nike said, pressing the microphone to her

lips. The sun beat down upon them. "Let's shut the canopies first. It's hotter than hell."

Once the canopies were locked down, Nike was able to turn on the air-conditioning. The coolness flowed past her helmeted face as they went through the preflight checklist in record time. The Apache quivered to life, its rotors swinging in slow arcs. Nike powered up and the blades began to churn. As she looked through the dark shield over her eyes, Nike snapped off a salute to the women on the ground. The chocks were removed from the wheels and they were ready to take off.

For the last two months, Nike had been able to fly the Apache exclusively. She loved being off the roster for assignments with the slow CH-47. As she placed her gloved hands around the cyclic and collective, she lifted the massive, deadly assault helo off the tarmac and into the air.

"I'm punching in the coordinates," Emma told her.

"Roger."

"I'm tuning us in to the A-team commo link so we can monitor them going in."

Lips compressed, Nike felt the helo moving powerfully through the desultory late-afternoon air. "Roger." The land grew distant as she brought the Apache up to seven thousand feet. With this bird, she didn't have to fly nap-of-the-earth. The Apache had every conceivable device on board to locate possible firing by the Taliban. This bird ruled the air in Afghanistan.

Her gaze flicked over the large panel in front of her. Nike watched airspeed and altitude and constantly craned her neck to spot problems. She heard scratchiness through the helmet earphones. Emma switched to the A-team frequency, which would enhance communication. In the past month, attacks on the army hunter-killer teams had escalated. They always did in the summer when travel was easier for both sides.

Her mind turned back to Gavin. She hadn't seen him in two months and was relieved he'd gone back into the field. After she'd dropped Jameela and Atefa into Kabul, her days of ferrying were over. Atefa now had a new leg and was doing fine.

The vibration moved through her hands and up into her arms. But despite her return to more comfortable surroundings, Nike couldn't stop thinking about Gavin. She felt the weight of the armored helicopter around her. Too bad she couldn't choose who to love. Not that she loved Gavin, but she kept seeing—feeling—that one, unexpected kiss in her mind. She'd replayed their conversations too many times to count. How sad was that? Nike could convince herself that she didn't care, but right now she admitted how worried she was for him and his team. It wasn't unusual to fly three missions a day in support of those out in the field. Each time the temptation came to nose around for Gavin and his men, she hesitated. Nike couldn't stop her dreams—the ones where she explored his body, her lips moulded against his, those strong hands ranging over her heated flesh. How many times had Nike awakened from sleep, breathing raggedly, aching for him? Too many.

They topped a mountain range, some snow left on the very tops, the blue-purple rock below. As they came over the valley, communications blared into her helmet.

"Red Dog One to Alpha One, over."

Nike gasped. *It was Gavin!* The moment she'd dreaded had come. Gavin's team was under attack!

"Alpha One this is Red Dog One, over," Emma's calm voice responded.

"We're getting another attack! I've got two men down.

One will die if I don't get medevac pronto! Do you have us in range? Over."

The desperation in his voice shook Nike as nothing else ever had. Hands tightening on the flight controls, she saw the puffs of mortars fired at a hill on the other side of the valley. She knew that the A teams set up lonely outposts in valleys to intercept the paths Taliban took into Afghanistan. Gavin must have been ordered to Alpha One. This valley was a hotbed of enemy attacks.

Pushing the Apache, Nike said, "I've got them in sight. Prepare the rockets."

"Roger," Emma said.

"Alpha One," Emma called, "we're on our way. Give me the coordinates of your position. Over."

Nike heard the back-and-forth between Emma and Gavin. The Apache screamed down out of the sky and Nike watched the firings at the top of the hill where Gavin and his team were pinned down. Her heart raced. Sweat trickled down the sides of her face as she brought the helicopter in line to fire the rockets.

"Ready and on target," Emma called.

Tension reigned in the cabin. "Fire at will," Nike said.

Instantly, the Apache shuddered as the first rocket left. Then a second, third and fourth. Nike watched with visceral pleasure as the rockets struck their targets. Rocks, dirt, flame and other debris exploded upward one, two, three and four times. The hill suddenly had tons of dirt gouged out of one side of it.

"On target!" Gavin yelled, triumph in his hoarse voice.

Emma continued to speak to the A-team leader. It was Nike's job to circle the entire hill. They had infrared aboard that would show body heat where the Taliban was hidden below in the tangle of thick brush. Emma also worked the infrared and continued to give her flight changes so that she could fire the Gatling gun beneath the belly of the helo at other pockets.

In moments, the Apache came on station and Nike held it at an angle, hovering about five hundred feet above a particularly thick grove of trees. Emma released a fusillade of fire, the Apache bucking beneath her hands as the Gatling gun spewed forth the bullets. Nike watched the bullets chew up the landscape like a shredder. Tree limbs exploded, bushes were torn up and she saw about twenty of the enemy scattering in all directions to get out of the line of fire.

It was then that Nike realized just how overwhelmed Gavin and his team had been. She estimated about a hundred of the enemy on all sides of the hill. Her headphones sang with communications between the team, Emma and ops. The sunlight lanced strongly into the cockpit and Nike didn't like it. This time of day was hard on the eyes, making it tougher to see. Fortunately, Nike had a television screen in front of her and she didn't have to crane her neck and squint. The television feed showed a number of other hiding places for the enemy.

Over the next five minutes, they systematically took the Taliban charge apart. The .45 pistol she carried on top of her flak jacket made it tough to draw in a deep breath of air. As Nike danced the Apache around the hill, they spotted another force of about fifty men coming down from the slope of a mountain behind the hill.

Whistling, she said, "They *want* to take that hill."

"No joke!" Emma said. "We're running low on ammo. Want to call in another Apache for support?"

"Roger that," Nike said grimly, and she switched the commo to another position to call ops with the request.

"Red Dog One, this is Alpha One," Nike said. She kept looking around as she brought the Apache to a thousand feet above the hill and continued to circle. This was the first time Gavin had heard her voice.

"Nike?"

She grinned. "Roger that, Red Dog One."

"I need immediate helo evacuation." Gavin's voice registered his surprise. "I've got one man with a severed artery. I've got a tourniquet on it but Burkie'll bleed out before the medevac can get here. Can you land, give up one of your seats and take him on board? Over."

The request was out of the ordinary and completely against regulations. Emma's gasp showed her shock, but what could they do? It would take forty minutes for medevac to arrive on station. By that time, his team member would be dead. Nike knew all the men, and her throat tightened. It was Emma's call. She was the XO. She had the position and power to override any rule.

"Emma?"

"I know," she said, her voice desperate. "Dammit!"

"We've got the Taliban on the run. The hill's clear and we've scattered the fifty coming down to join them. I think we'll be okay to land. We can do this before our backup arrives."

"Are you volunteering to stay behind?"

Nike hadn't thought that far. "I guess I am. Can you clear this request and give permission?" she begged.

"We shouldn't do this," Emma said grimly. "It's against our orders. Dallas will hang us."

"I know, but there's a man dying down there. There's enough room to land and take off, Emma. I can set this girl down, hop out and we can get the guy on board. It'll be easy for you to fly him back at top speed. I don't think the Taliban will regroup. We've killed most of them."

Nike held her breath. If Emma approved the illegal pickup and leaving a pilot behind, it was her ass on the line. Emma was one hell of a pilot and a damn good leader. If anyone could persuade Dallas this was the right decision, it would be Emma.

"Okay, okay, let's get down there. I'm going to rig some static for a call to ops requesting permission. They won't give it to us, but we'll pretend we heard otherwise."

Nike wanted to cry for joy. "We'll stick together on this."

Chuckling, Emma said, "We're BJS and crazy wild women, anyway. This might not be in the flight rules for the boys flying Apaches, but for us, it's no rules at times. Peru taught us that."

Nike understood. How many times down in Peru were the flight book and rules thrown out the window? Too many times to count. If nothing else, BJS was a fly-by-the-seat-of-your-pants squadron. It shouldn't be any different here, either.

"Red Dog One, this is Alpha One. Clear off an area north of your position on the hilltop. We're coming in to land. Once down, I have to shut off the engines. Bring your man once the blades have stop turning. Over."

"Thank you, Alpha One. We'll get on it pronto. Out."

Nike heard the incredible relief in Gavin's voice. Knowing how tight he was with his men, that they were family to him, Nike felt moisture in her eyes. She blinked away tears as she noted the men scrambling to the north end of the hill to pick up anything that the blades might kick into the air. If there was anything lying around, the power of the blades could throw it up in the air and turn it into weapons against them.

Emma rigged the shorting-out communications call with ops and made it sound like static. She laughed darkly. "Okay, we're indicted now. Ready to land?"

"Yes."

Banking the Apache, Nike swooped down and brought the helo to a hover fifty feet above the clearing.

"You can take a hop back on the medevac that's already under way."

"Roger that. No way do I want to stay on that hilltop tonight." Nike brought the Apache down until its tri-wheels hunkered on the earth. Dust clouds kicked up in every direction until the blades had stopped. She pushed open the canopy, climbed out and leaped to the ground.

Two men were carrying a third between them. The injured man's left leg had a tourniquet, midthigh. Blood stained his entire pant leg down to his boot. Gavin trotted up, his face grim, rifle in hand. There were splotches of blood all over his uniform. He'd probably dragged his friend out of the line of fire.

Emma had thrown open her cockpit canopy and stood on the seat to give the men directions.

Nike met Gavin's eyes and ached for the fear and grimness in them. He handed her the rifle and then lithely leaped up on the Apache. Together, the three men got the unconscious soldier into the cockpit. Nike watched as Gavin quickly harnessed him up. Within two minutes, Emma was ready to take off. Gavin locked the canopy back into place and gave her a thumbs-up.

Nike handed Gavin his weapon as he leaped off the Apache. Together, they all moved away.

"Are you all right?" Gavin demanded as they stood back and hunkered down.

"I'm fine."

"Thanks for doing this," he said.

"No problem." She was kneeling down in a foxhole dug deeply enough to keep them hidden. The dust from the Apache kicked up and the shriek of the engines was like music to her ears. Coughing, Nike shut her eyes and covered her mouth as the thick dust rolled by.

Within three minutes, the Apache was hotfooting it across the valley toward base. The thunking sound of the blades beat in echoing retreats across the valley. Nike told Gavin that a medevac was on the way, and Gavin nodded. "That's good to hear. You're going to be on it."

"Yes, I will be."

He wiped the sweat off his brow. His hands trembled as he put another clip of ammo into his weapon. "You just saved our bacon. At least a hundred of those bastards were down there."

"I'm glad we made the difference." Nike sat down in the hole, dust all over her flight suit. She saw the rest of the men in other foxholes across the top of the hill. Huge craters had formed from mortars fired earlier by the Taliban. The sun slanted powerfully across the hill, making it difficult to see on the western side.

"I've got two other men wounded, but they're walking and firing." He locked and loaded his weapon, craned his neck out of the hole and gazed down the side of the chewed-up hill. Sitting back down, he conferred with his assistant and told him to keep watch, this was merely a lull in the fighting.

Nike sat next to him, her heart lifting with joy to see him alive. "How long have you been up here?"

"Too long. It's been twenty-eight days so far, Nike." He managed a grin. "Why? Do I smell bad?"

Nike chuckled. "This isn't exactly the Ritz."

"I'd give almost anything for a hot shower." He met and held her gaze. "But right now, I'm the happiest man on earth. You're here. With me. Amazing."

Laughing softly, Nike said, "Okay, I missed you a little, too."

"Really?"

She liked the amusement in his crinkled eyes. "A *little,*" she stressed. Right now, Gavin looked more like an eagle on the hunt than the laid-back soldier she'd met at base camp two months ago. She reminded herself that he'd been under attack, his adrenaline was up and he was in survival mode.

Gavin wanted to grab Nike and crush her against him. He could smell the shampoo she'd used this morning in her hair. Any fragrance compared to the hell he'd seen on this hill over the last three weeks was welcome.

"Are you wounded?" she said, pointing to his leg. Besides being dirty and torn, he had some fresh blood on his right thigh.

"What? Oh, that. I'm fine. It was just some shrapnel from a mortar."

"You should be medevaced out, too."

"No way."

Frowning, Nike began to really study the rest of the team. They were all wounded to some degree and oblivious to it. All their attention was riveted on the base of the hill where the next attack might come from. The courage these men displayed amazed her.

"How long has this attack been going on?"

"Four days off and on. Today they attacked en masse,"

Gavin said. He pulled out a canteen and guzzled water. Droplets leaked out the corners of his mouth and down his beard. After finishing, he looked over at her. "They want this hill back. From here, we can see everything going on in this valley. Since we got here over three weeks ago, we've called in ten strikes on them as they tried to cross the valley at night to get into Afghanistan."

"No wonder they're pissed," she said, giving him a grin. His blue eyes lightened for a moment and Nike could feel his desire. She could almost feel it surrounding her. And then, he glanced away and the moment was broken. She wanted those seconds back.

"Yeah, just a little." He stretched his head up above the hole to study the slope for a moment. "I'm glad you're going to be out of here by dark."

"Why?"

"They'll attack then. Damn good thing we have night scopes to pick up their body-heat signatures or we'd have been dead up here a long time ago."

He said it so matter-of-factly, and yet, for Nike, the words were a shock to her system. Gavin Jackson dead. For the first time, it really struck her that it could happen. Before, Nike had felt he was such a confident leader, that nothing could bring him down. Now, sitting here in a foxhole with him, she felt very different. And she was scared to death.

Chapter 9

There was nothing to do but wait. Nike remained in the foxhole while Gavin made his rounds, running and ducking into the next foxhole to speak with his men. Their only communication was by yelling. He and his second-in-command had radios, but that was it.

Nike kept cautiously peeking over the top of the foxhole, watching below and wondering if they'd destroyed enough of the enemy to keep them at bay for another hour. She wasn't sure. Wiping her mouth, which tasted of dust, she took one of the canteens in the foxhole and drank some water.

Luckily for her, she had her radio and could remain in contact with ops and any flights coming their way. Still, she felt dread. Was this how Gavin and his men felt all the time? The waiting? The wondering when the next attack would come? She couldn't conceive of living in this type of nonstop stress. Her admiration for the A team rose accordingly.

The top of the hill was about the size of a football field, although rounded. The hill was steep and not easy to climb. There had been a wooden lookout at one time, but it had been splintered into oblivion by repeated by enemy mortar rounds. The scrub bush that coated the sides of the hill was massive and thick. Nike had seen it from the air and knew men could quietly sneak up almost to the edge of the top of the hill. Her adrenaline pounded through her. What would happen at night?

She could hear Gavin's voice drifting her way from time to time. The foxholes were deep and the nine remaining men stayed in a circle at the top so intruders could be spotted coming from any direction. The afternoon sun was nearly gone and was dipping behind the peaks. As much as she tried to stifle it, Nike was scared for all of them, not just herself.

When Gavin leaped back into the hole, she noticed he'd put his Afghan hat back on. He wore body armor beneath the dusty white shirt, soaked with sweat beneath his armpits. It gave him a little protection from flying bullets.

"Like my digs?" he asked casually, putting his weapon next to him and taking another swig from one of the canteens.

"This is a special hell," Nike said, frowning. Searching his sweaty, dirty face, she added, "I don't know how you take this kind of stress."

"It's not fun," Gavin admitted, twisting the cap back on his water.

"Has this hill been a U.S. outlook for some time?"

"Yes. And with great regularity the Taliban drops mortars on it hoping to kill us." He gestured toward where the wooden tower had once stood. "We build the look-out tower and they come back and bomb it to oblivion."

She shook her head. "I never realized the kind of danger you were in."

"No one does until they're up to their butts in it," Gavin said, grinning. He took his weapon and made sure there was a round in the chamber. With the rag in his pocket, he tried to clean most of the dust off the weapon.

"Will they attack?" Nike asked.

"I don't know. Depends upon how much damage you were able to do to them."

"Do they attack every day?"

"No, but since two days ago, they've made a concerted effort to take back this hill." Gavin made circular gestures above his head. "This hill is the key to the whole valley, Nike. It sits at one end and with our binoculars and infrared scope, we can see anyone trying to cross it at night."

"How are you being resupplied?"

"We aren't," he said, frowning. "We're low on ammo and water. Usually, we get a flight in here twice a week. We're in dire need of resupply right now."

"And you can't get it because…?"

"The Taliban keep firing at the helicopter transport that's supposed to supply us. Oh, there's always an Apache with it and they lay down fire, but this time, it hasn't worked. If the transport can't land to resupply us, well…"

"Have you made a call to your commander about this?" She felt her throat tighten with concern.

Gavin wiped his brow with the back of his arm. "Yes." He looked at his watch. "I figure in about twenty minutes we should see a medevac, a transport and an Apache come flying in."

"Then what?"

"Well, we're going to swap out A teams. A fresh team will come in with supplies and we'll be airlifted out of here."

Relief spread through Nike. "That's good news."

Grunting, he said, "Not for the team coming in. It's one of the hot spots on the border and no one wants this assignment."

Nike gulped. "Is anyone else in your team injured besides yourself?"

"Oh, we all are more or less," Gavin said.

Nike couldn't believe how calm he was about it all. She noticed again the dark red blood that had stained half the trouser across his right thigh. "Are you okay? It looks like your wound is bleeding more."

"I caught a flesh wound," he said. "It's nothing. I'll be okay."

She sat there digesting all the information. "I never realized how…dangerous…"

Chuckling, Gavin reached out and patted her shoulder. "Hey, it's okay. You Airedales fly above the fray. It's ground-pounding soldiers like us who stare eyeball to eyeball with the bad guys."

His touch felt so good. Suddenly, Nike realized just how much she liked Gavin. Despite the terror, the trauma and the possibility of another attack, he was joking and seemingly at ease about his lot in life. This was real courage.

"You're right, Gavin. I sit up there and I'm not connected to the ground below."

"Well, saves you a lot of PTSD symptoms," he told her wryly. He sat with the rifle between his drawn-up legs, arms around it.

"That's not even funny," she muttered.

"You know what I do when things are quiet like this?"

She heard a wistful note in his voice. "No. What?"

"I think about you. About us."

A bit of ruddiness crept across his cheeks. It was hard to believe that Gavin would blush but he did. "Us?" Her pulse started as he gave her a warm look.

"Yeah." Looking around at the foxhole and then up at the blue sky, Gavin said, "It helps me hold on. When things are bad, I remember that kiss."

So did she, but she wasn't about to admit it. "Oh."

Gavin gave her an assessing look and added, "I swore that if we got off this hill alive, I was going to hunt you down."

A thrill moved through her, though Nike tried to stay neutral. "This isn't fair, Gavin."

"What isn't?"

"You know my past. I lost the man I loved to an enemy bullet. I can't go through that again."

Hearing the desperation in her voice, Gavin reached out and gripped her hand. "Hey, life is dangerous. Not just to military people, but to everyone."

"Especially to the military." Nike jerked her hand out of his. She felt stifled and trapped. Her heart yearned for Gavin, but her past experience had done too much damage. Nike pleaded, "I'm afraid to love anyone in the military ever again, Gavin." There, the truth was out.

Gavin absorbed her strained words. Every once in a while, he'd look up and over the crater to peruse the hill below, but everything seemed quiet. "I appreciate your honesty, Nike. A lot of people allow fear to run their lives in different ways. There's the woman who won't leave a marriage because she fears losing the security. There's the man who fears leaving his job for another one." Shaking his head, he held her narrowed golden gaze. "Fear is every-where all the time, Nike."

"What do you fear?"

He smiled. "Being alone. See? I have my fear, too."

"Why fear being alone?" She searched his pensive face.

"My mother nearly died when I was a little kid. As a ten-year-old I lived through days and nights when she didn't come home from the hospital. My father tried to help me, but I felt this terror that I'd never see her again. She'd had appendicitis with complications, but as a young kid, I didn't realize what had happened. My father, bless him, tried to keep the three of us cared for, but he had a job. We ended up with a babysitter and not a very good one at that."

"It would be hard for a young child to have a parent suddenly gone from their lives like that."

"It was. I look back on that time a lot. My mom nearly died, but my father never let on how bad it was. I was in school, and that helped. I used to come home and look for her, thinking she was playing a game of hide-and-seek with me."

Nike's heart ached for his pain. "That must have been very hard on everyone."

Picking up a clod of dirt, Gavin crushed it in his fist and let the soil sift between his fingers. "That was one of the most defining moments of my life. I felt abandoned and afraid."

"But she survived?"

Nodding, Gavin said, "Yes, she came back ten days later. We couldn't visit her in the hospital because of the type of infection she had. And she was in a coma, so we couldn't talk to her on the phone. My dad kept telling us she was all right, but none of us believed that."

"Wow," Nike whispered, "that was awful for her and you kids."

He leaned back against the dirt wall. "Yeah, it was. And when she did come home, she was very weak. Nothing like the mother I had known before. I don't know who cried more—us or her when she was brought in the door on a gurney by the ambulance crew."

Nike sat digesting it all. "And she did recover?"

"Fully. It took about six months though. She looked like a skeleton and we all thought she was going to die. My father lost his job because he had to stay home and take care of us. We didn't have the money for a full-time babysitter or a nurse. I remember waking up with nightmares." He sighed. "It was always the same nightmare—Mom was dead. I'd go into her room and she'd be on the bed, dead."

"How awful." Reaching out, she let her hand fall over his. She could feel the grit of dust beneath her fingertips. "I'm so sorry, Gavin."

He enclosed her fingers and gave them a gentle squeeze. "Hey, every family has their trauma and heartache."

"That's true," Nike admitted. Her hand tingled over Gavin's touch. She couldn't deny any longer she was powerfully drawn to him. "So how did this affect your life?"

Gavin chuckled and made another quick check down the slope on their side of the hill. Sitting down, he said, "My fear is abandonment. My whole life has revolved around the possibility of loss. When I joined Special Forces after graduating, I made damn sure I would never abandon my men or leave them without help."

"Unlike the ten-year-old who was abandoned by his mom?"

"Yep." Gavin sighed. "And I got into some pretty stupid relationships with women because of it, too."

"You wouldn't abandon them?"

"No, but they abandoned me in many different ways. I always seem to pick strong women who have no problem having affairs with other men."

"Ouch," Nike murmured. "That has to hurt."

"Yeah."

"Did that ever stop you from having a relationship?"

Giving her a warm look, Gavin said, "Oh, it would for a while, but then I'd jump back into the fray and choose the same kind of woman all over again."

"I don't see how you could keep going back and trying again," she said.

"What's the other choice? Becoming a monk in a cave in the Himalayas?"

Nike laughed along with him, feeling the connection to him deepen. "Well, at least you have the guts and courage to jump back in and try. I don't."

"Maybe you just needed time," Gavin said.

"Two years."

He shrugged. "Well, everyone is different, Nike. Was Antonio the first man you've fallen in love with?"

She nodded. "Coming from a strict Greek upbringing, I was taught that love comes along only once. My parents have been married since their twenties. They're very much in love with one another to this day. I wanted that for myself. I wanted that happiness."

"But it isn't working out that way for you."

Nike nodded. "I used to think happiness would just happen."

"I don't think happiness is a guarantee in our life," Gavin said ruefully.

"No," Nike said grimly, looking up at the darkening sky. "That's how I see it now."

"So your world view got shattered when he died."

"Just like yours did when you were ten."

"Life does things to all of us," Gavin said. "I guess what I got out of my mother and father was that hope springs eternal. He never gave up on her. He would hold us, promise us that she was coming home. For whatever reason, the ten-year-old me wanted to see her before I would believe him."

"You can't be hard on yourself. You were only ten, scared, and suddenly you had your mom ripped out of your life."

"I learned then that nothing in life is safe."

"You're right about that." Nike sighed. She sat digesting his words. *Nothing is safe.* Sitting here in a foxhole on a hill in Afghanistan proved that. "I feel safe when I'm flying an Apache."

"That's only because you haven't ever been shot down."

"Mmm," she agreed. Rubbing her brow, Nike gave him a frustrated look. "I'm too much of an idealist. I think everything is safe and fine until it blows up in my face."

"Right," Gavin murmured. "But we all get those left hooks that life gives us. The point is to get back up, dust off your britches and move back into the fray."

"And you've done it time and again."

Gavin nodded. "Yes, I have."

"Don't you get tired? Exhausted?"

"Sure I do." He gave her an uneven grin. "But then, hope infuses me, and I start all over again. I open back up and do the best I can."

Rubbing her armor-clad chest, Nike confided, "You're a far braver person that I have ever been, Gavin."

He looked at his watch. "I have an idea."

"What?"

"We happen to like each other. In about ten minutes, those helos will be flying into the valley. How about when we get back to base, we start all over?"

Nike felt fear along with a burst of elation. "What are you talking about?"

"My team will get two weeks' R & R. I'd like to get to know you when things aren't as frantic or dramatic as they are right now. Can we get together and just talk?" He opened his hands and grinned wolfishly. "I promise, I won't hit on you. Maybe what you need is a gentle transfer from the fear of losing someone into making friends once more."

"I don't know, Gavin."

"Look at us," he said persuasively. "We're sitting here in a foxhole together just talking. I like hearing about your life and how you see things. I know you're enjoying yourself."

"Yes, I am."

"This proves that we can be friends."

"That's not what you really want," she challenged, feeling that old panic again.

"No, but I can be satisfied with friendship, Nike. In all my other relationships, I never had what we have. I like it. My parents used to tell me that the strongest base for a relationship was being friends first. I'm just now, with you, beginning to understand that statement."

"You were never friends with the women in your life?"

"Not really. And that's where I may have made a huge mistake."

Uneasy, Nike said, "Antonio and I were the best of friends." She saw him digest that statement.

"Maybe," he said, a bit of wistfulness in his tone, "you're the best thing ever to happen to me."

Quirking her mouth, Nike said, "I wouldn't be so sure of that."

Gavin heard the sounds of rotors and craned his neck to the west. "Oh, I am. Hey, here comes our rescue party. Two Apaches. That's even better."

About that time, Gavin's radio blared to life. Nike heard her CO's voice. Dallas was flying one of the Apaches, which meant she and Emma were probably in a helluva lot of hot water. And Dallas was on the flight schedule today. She'd soon find out.

Gavin gave directions to the medevac and transport, a CH-47, about where to land on the hilltop. Before they did, the Apaches made a sweep of the entire area to ensure the transport could land without being fired upon. For the next ten minutes, the two Apaches used their infrared cameras to look for warm bodies in the area. There were none.

Gavin stood up as the CH-47 came in for a landing. Holding out his hand, he said, "Come on, Nike. We get to go home—together."

She gripped his hand and stood up. Standing there, rifle on his shoulder, he looked incredibly strong and courageous. If nothing else, Nike felt like a true coward in comparison. Right now, she had her CO to worry about. If Emma couldn't sell the reason for letting off the pilot to take an injured soldier on board, her career could be in real jeopardy. Watching the CH-47 hover and slowly come down, Nike wasn't sure what to expect.

Chapter 10

Once Gavin had helped her onto the ramp of the CH-47, he backed away, which surprised her. The other A team trundled off and quickly left the area of the rotor blades. Some of Gavin's A team came on board and the rest went on the medevac. Nike turned, confused.

"I'll see you back at base tomorrow," he called, stepping away.

The ramp started to grind and groan as it came up. Nike realized that Gavin was probably going to fill in the next team and she sat down. She dutifully put on the helmet, but couldn't shake the disappointment that he wasn't coming back with her. She understood why, but it didn't help her fear. The Taliban could attack again. At night.

The CH-47 lifted off, the shuddering familiar and comforting. Closing her eyes, she leaned back and tried to relax. The pilot would be doing the roller-coaster nap-of-the-earth flying, and she hung on. Her mind turned to consider the inevitable: Dallas Klein, her CO, was probably pissed off as hell at what she and Emma had done. They'd broken every cardinal rule in the Apache flight book. Who knew what kind of punishment Dallas would dole out?

The moment Nike stepped into the BJS 60 headquarters, the staff looked up, their expressions grim. A sergeant, Carolyn Cannon, said, "Major Klein wants to see you right away, Captain Alexander."

I'll bet she does. Nike nodded. Normally, Emma Trayhern-Cantrell, the XO of the squadron, would have been at her desk, but there was no sign of her. Girding herself, Nike marched up to the closed door, knocked once and heard "Enter." Compressing her lips, Nike gripped the doorknob, twisted it and entered.

To her surprise, Emma stood at rigid attention in front of Major Klein's desk. Cutting her gaze to her CO, Nike knew she was in a lot of trouble. The older woman's eyes blazed with rage.

Coming to the front of the desk, Nike said, "Reporting as ordered, ma'am." Sweat began to gather on her brow and her heart pounded with adrenaline. Nike had never seen Dallas this angry.

"Captain, what the *hell* were you thinking when you left the cockpit of your Apache? You know damn well neither pilot is to *ever* leave that helicopter for *any* reason unless it's on fire."

Nike looked straight ahead to the wall behind her CO. "Ma'am, Berkie…er…Sergeant Berkland Hall, the communications sergeant, was bleeding to death. Captain Jackson said he'd die before a medevac got there to rescue him. Berkie…er…Sergeant Hall's wife had their first child three months ago. I—I didn't want to see him die. I wanted

to see him live to get home to see his new baby. Ma'am…"
Right now, that all sounded like a decision based on too
many emotions, but Nike stuck to her guns.

"Captain Trayhern-Cantrell says she ordered you out of
the cockpit. Is that true?" Dallas growled.

Gut clenching, Nike realized Emma was being true to
her word to take the fall on this breaking of rules. Nike
didn't want to leave Emma at the center of the problem.
"Er… Ma'am, it was a mutual decision."

"Mutual?" Dallas yelled. She glared at Emma. "Dammit,
you're XO of this squadron! You have no business making
any 'mutual' decisions!"

Emma shot a fearful glance at Nike and then said, "Yes,
ma'am."

Dallas got up and prowled the small office, glaring at
both women. "I have my XO, who is supposed to be the
poster child for following rules, breaking them. And then I
have one of my best pilots agreeing with her to break those
rules, too." Hands behind her dark green flight suit, Dallas
stalked around her desk.

"There are men dying out there every day, ladies. We
are not medevac. If you want to be medevac you should
have damned well volunteered to do that kind of service
work. Our job—" and she punched an index finger in their
direction "—is to protect and defend. The Apache is *not* a
medevac!"

Swinging her attention to Emma, she added, "Dammit,
Trayhern-Cantrell, what if you'd got shot coming back?
What if you'd needed Nike on the instruments if the Taliban
started firing at you? What if, God forbid, we'd needed the
two of you on another call on the way back?"

"You're right, ma'am," Emma whispered contritely.

"I don't want to be right!" Dallas exploded. "I want you

to know what is right, Captain! You're a damn poor example for our squadron. It makes all of us look bad."

Emma's lips thinned and she said nothing, her eyes straight ahead.

Nike cringed inwardly. In all her years knowing Dallas as the XO of the Black Jaguar Squadron down in Peru, she'd never seen her fly off the handle as she was doing. That was how serious this was, Nike realized. At the time, it had seemed like the right decision to make. She didn't know yet if Berkie had survived or not. She'd come straight here to HQ from the helo.

"Of all the harebrained decisions the two of you have ever made, this goes over the top." Dallas glared at them. "What am I to do? If I don't punish you for your decision, then one of my other pilots will get it into her head that it's okay to climb out of the cockpit on a mission to give up her seat to another injured soldier."

Wincing, Nike felt the blast of her CO's anger. Oh, it was justified. The only question now was what Dallas Klein was going to do to punish them for their blatant transgression. She could feel two spots burning into her cheeks as her CO watched her.

"All right," Dallas flared, her voice suddenly deadly quiet, "neither of you leave me any choice. Captain Trayhern-Cantrell, you're stripped of your status as XO. You've just proven you aren't up to the task of reinforcing the rules that we must all live under here in combat."

Nike winced. She knew that punishment would go on Emma's personnel jacket and it could stop her from making major someday. There was nothing Nike could do about it, and she felt terrible.

"Yes, ma'am," Emma croaked, shock in her tone.

"Remember, Trayhern-Cantrell, you did this to yourself.

You made the decision! You shouldn't have allowed that A team captain to influence you as he did. You've clearly shown that you don't have the backbone to enforce the rules."

"Yes, ma'am," Emma whispered.

Heart breaking, Nike heard the pain in Emma's tone. She knew that Emma came from a military dynasty, a very famous one. There were so many medals and awards for valor in the Trayhern family, and now Emma was giving it a black eye. Emma must feel awful about this. Guiltily, Nike knew it had been her idea to pick up Berkie.

"Ma'am," Nike spoke up strongly, "Emma is innocent in all of this! I—"

"That's not true, ma'am," Emma piped up quickly, giving her friend a panicked look.

"Quiet!"

Nike grimly shut up, as did Emma. Her attempt to save her friend was not going to work. When Dallas had been a young pilot, she had to have made some stupid decisions, too. She'd probably been in a similar situation herself.

Breathing hard, Dallas said, "Do you realize what you've done? We're a covert black ops. We've come here with an incredibly spotless record of positive work as an all-female squadron. And you two decide to screw it up with this stupid, completely avoidable mistake."

Nike'd known the chewing-out was going to be bad, but not this bad. She felt guilty that her desire to save Berkie would give all the women of this squadron a bad name, but still couldn't be sorry for her action. Her decision broke the rules, but wasn't wrong by moral standards. With that resolve, Nike was prepared for the worst. What made it tough was how Emma selflessly threw herself under the bus. She didn't have to, but she did. Nike felt awful about that.

"What the hell am I going to do with the two of you?" Dallas spat. "It isn't like I have women pilots standing in line to fly Apaches! But I can't trust the two of you in the cockpit, either." Glaring at them, Dallas shook her head.

"I'm sorry, ma'am." Emma's voice was quiet and apologetic.

Nike absorbed the brittle tension that hung in the small office. She was sure the office pogues outside could hear everything. It was completely unlike Dallas to scream at anyone like this.

"Captain Trayhern-Cantrell, you're demoted. It will be reflected in your jacket and haunt you for the rest of your military life. You have not done your proud military family any favors with your poor decision-making. From now on, you will be just one of the pilots in the squadron. One slip-up—and I mean *one*—and I'll send your ass back to the States and you can be reassigned into a mixed-gender helicopter squadron flying transports. You got that?"

"Yes, ma'am."

Nike tensed inwardly as Dallas swung her glare to her.

"And you, Captain Alexander. I have a terrible feeling this was all your idea and that Captain Trayhern-Cantrell was the patsy for your desire to help that man. War is not pretty. I thought you would have got that in Peru, but obviously, you didn't. You let your compassion for that man affect your judgment. I can no longer trust you in the cockpit of an Apache, can I?"

"No, ma'am, I guess you can't," Nike whispered.

"There's no *guess* about it, Captain Alexander." Dallas fumed. "Dammit, you leave me no choice. From now on the only time you'll have your ass strapped into an Apache is to keep up your flight skills. I'm assigning you permanently to the transport squadron here on base until you can be trusted to fly an Apache properly. I need every woman I have to man the Apaches and you've now left me a pilot short. I'm calling back to the Pentagon to see if I can find another female pilot to replace you."

Nike closed her eyes, taking her CO's words like punches. She had never anticipated this. Her Apache days were over. "Yes, ma'am," she croaked.

"I can't trust you, Captain Alexander. That's what this really comes down to, isn't it?"

It was useless to try and fight for herself. "Yes, ma'am," Nike said.

"Has it ever occurred to you that I could court-martial you, drum you out of the the U.S. Army and send you back to Greece?"

Horrified, Nike opened her mouth and then snapped it shut. The fury in Dallas's eyes burned through her.

"I could do that, Captain. But dammit, that would be another blow to BJS 60 and frankly, I don't want that on our record. I wanted to make a positive record of our performance as an all-woman squadron here in Afghanistan. So you're safe on that score and damn lucky," she gritted out.

Closing her eyes, Nike swallowed hard. She opened them and stared straight ahead at the light green wall behind her CO. "Thank you, ma'am."

Dallas sat down. She scribbled out a set of orders. "Captain Alexander, you're officially transferred to the transport squadron based here. All you are going to do is fly CH-47s. Maybe that will remind you of your bad choices and how you've hurt our squadron. Fly with those realities in mind." She thrust the papers at Nike. "Now, both of you, get out of here. Dismissed."

"I'm sorry," Nike told Emma once they were back in their tent area. The night was dark and they had their flashlights. "I didn't think…."

Emma put her arm around Nike's slumped shoulders. "I'm sorry, too. I don't care if I lose the XO position. I know the rules are there for a reason. We made a choice and got caught, was all."

"There were times in Peru when we would take a sick child or adult out of a village and fly them to Cusco," Nike grumbled. "And Dallas damn well knew we did it. We'd leave one of the pilots behind, radio in to the cave and let them know what we were doing and nothing was ever said by Dallas or the CO."

"Yes, but it's different here," Emma said. "Down there, we had no other military ops around us. Here, the eyes of the whole base watch our every move because we're an all-female squadron."

"Humph," Nike growled. They stepped carefully through the ruts made by a storm the night before. "Dallas knows we did that stuff down there."

"Yes, but she's CO now. And the men are watching us," Emma said. "Dallas didn't have a choice in this and I knew it."

Giving her friend a sharp glance, Nike said, "You knew she'd bust you out of XO position?"

Giving her a slight smile, Emma nodded. "Sure. That's what I would have done if I was CO. I was just hoping she wouldn't have been so hard on you, that she'd put a reprimand in your personnel file and let it go at that."

"Dallas knows I was the one who thought it up, that's why."

Halting at a row of tents, they turned. It was chow time and most of the women were gone. Nike was glad. Word would spread like wildfire. By morning, the whole camp would be aware of their new orders.

"I'm not hungry," Emma said, halting in front of her tent, next to Nike's. "Are you?"

Nike laughed sourly. "The only thing I want is a stiff damn drink of pisco to burn out the tension in my gut."

Emma grinned. Pisco was the drink of Peru. It could kick like a mule once it was gulped down. "Yeah, that sounds pretty good right now. I'll bet Dallas has a stash of it hidden somewhere."

Nike's spirits rose over her indomitable friend. "I don't think she's going to share it with us, do you?"

Giggling, Emma said in a whisper, "Not a chance."

"I'm going over to the med tent," Nike told her. "I don't even know if Berkie made it or not."

"He was in terrible shape," Emma admitted quietly. She put her hand on Nike's shoulder. "I'm going to lie down and try to sleep. I feel like I was in a dogfight and lost."

Nike nodded. "Yeah, it hurts, doesn't it? Well, we did this to ourselves. Dallas did what she had to do."

"Gosh, Nike, you can only fly CH-47s now. That's terrible! I never thought Dallas would go that far."

"I know," Nike whispered glumly. "What bothers me is that if she replaces me, I'll never get back into the squadron. I could finish out my tour here in Afghanistan flying transports. That sucks."

Emma nodded. "Putting an aggressive combat pilot to fly a bus is a horrible punishment."

"It could have been worse," Nike reminded her solemnly.

"Well, all we can do is be good pilots from here on out and do the best we can. Over time, this thing will settle out and be forgotten."

"I hope so," Nike said. What would she tell her parents? They would be shocked. "I still am not sorry we did it, Emma."

"I'm not, either," Emma told her. "If Dallas knew that, she *would* court-martial us."

Depressed, Nike agreed. "Well, it's our secret for the rest of our lives. We can't tell our families, either. You know how word gets around.…"

"Mmm," Emma agreed. "My dad is going to hit the roof and God, my mom is going to be scraped off the ceiling, too. And my uncle Morgan is going to…well, who knows what he'll do.…"

Nike knew that Clay and Aly were very proud of their daughter. The Trayhern family created warriors for the military and Emma was no slouch. She was one of the finest Apache pilots ever to go through the school. And her uncle, Morgan Trayhern, was a genuine military hero who was highly respected within that world. "I'm really sorry about that."

Emma shrugged. "They'll understand. I'm not sure Uncle Morgan will, but I know my parents will forgive me and just tell me to keep my head down and do good work."

"What do you think your uncle will do?" Morgan Trayhern was in a position of power running a black-ops company that helped the U.S. government in many different ways.

"Ugh, I don't know."

"He has influence," Nike said hopefully. "Do you think

there's anything he can do to help you take the black mark out of your jacket?"

Emma placed her hands on her hips and looked up at the stars overhead. "Probably not. He'll probably agree with Major Klein's decision. He's not a rule-breaker, Nike."

Nike snorted. "I'll bet he broke plenty of rules when he was in the military. He just didn't get caught like we did, is all."

"Listen, head on over to the clinic. Find out about Berkie. I sure hope he made it."

"I'll let you know." Nike opened her arms and impulsively hugged Emma. "Thanks for everything. If Berkie made it, it's because of you."

Releasing her, Emma grinned. "Let me know, okay? Come back, and if I'm sleeping, wake me up?"

Nike watched as a medic behind the desk rifled through a bunch of papers. He then consulted the computer, scanning for the name Berkland Hall.

"Yes, ma'am, he's alive," the young blond medic finally said as he tapped the computer screen. "He's resting in stable condition at the hospital at Bagram Air Force Base. Says here they're going to be transporting him back to the States tomorrow morning."

"Thank you," Nike said, relief in her tone. She left the busy medic tent and headed back out into the darkness. Tears burned her eyes. Berkie would live to see his newly born daughter. His wife would have a husband. A sob ripped from her and Nike pressed her hand against her mouth, afraid that someone nearby might hear her. She couldn't cry here.

There was a spot on the north side of the base where Nike went to sit and clear her head. This night, after this horrible day, she went to her rock, turned off her flashlight and simply allowed the darkness to swallow her up. She loved looking at the myriad stars since they reminded her of her home in Greece. Right now, she felt alone and depressed. And she worried about Gavin, hoping the Taliban weren't attacking the hill tonight. Because she was between squadrons, there was no way for her to know. Until she took her orders to the new CO of the transport squadron, she couldn't ask anyone about anything.

Touching the BJS 60 patch on her right shoulder, Nike knew she'd have to take it off tomorrow before going to the CO of the transport squadron at 0800. For all intents and purposes, she had been drummed out of BJS 60 in shame. She wrapped her arms around her drawn-up legs. She had no one to thank for this but herself. Inside, she was a mass of contradictory emotions. Berkie was alive because they'd broken the rules. A little baby and a wife would have a father and husband to complete their lives. It had been a hell of a decision, and Nike didn't mind paying for it personally. She hated that Emma had stepped in and taken part of the blame, but that was Emma. Nike had often seen her wearing the mantle of the Trayhern dynasty and sometimes, it weighed heavily on her. *What a mess.* Nike had ended up getting Emma's fine career smeared permanently.

It all seemed overwhelming in that moment. She balanced out her grief over the decisions that Major Klein had made against Berkie being alive. What was a life worth? Everything, in Nike's mind. Lifting her chin, she saw a meteor flash across the night sky. How was Gavin? Was he safe? When would he fly back here to be with his team?

Nike realized that she truly missed Gavin. The wonderful, searching talk they'd had last night was burned into her heart's memory. She was such a coward when it came to trusting love.

Love?

Snorting, Nike released her arms from around her knees and stood up. *Am I falling in love with Gavin? No, that couldn't be.* Hadn't she been punished enough in one day's time? Did she need this awareness like a curse upon her, too?

Shaking her head, Nike couldn't assimilate all of the day's unexpected turns and twists. Yet, as she turned and shuffled back toward the tent city hidden in the darkness, Nike still missed Gavin. If he was here, she could confide in him. He would understand. Right now, Nike ached to have his arms around her. Right now, she needed to be held....

Chapter 11

Gavin sat in the medical-facility tent on a gurney. The doctor had cut away most of his blood-soaked pant leg, inspected the bullet wound that had created a three-inch gash across his thigh. The place was a beehive of activity this morning. It was raining and he was soaked after coming off a helo that had brought him back to the base.

"Well?" Gavin asked Dr. Hartman, a young black-haired man with blue eyes.

"Flesh wound. You're lucky, Captain Jackson," Dr. Hartman said, looking up.

"Shoot me full of antibiotics, sew me up and authorize me back to my team," he told the doctor.

Hartman grinned a little. A female army nurse came over with a tray that held the antibiotic, a syringe, needle and thread plus some scrubbing material to ensure that the wound was free of debris. "I know how you A-teamers like to stick together, Captain," Hartman said, picking up a syringe that would locally anesthetize the wound area first.

"It's just a flesh wound," Gavin said. He sat on the gurney, his good leg hanging over the side. While the army would give him three weeks at the base to let the wound heal properly, Gavin didn't want it. His team would be ordered out without him and that bothered him greatly. He felt protective of his men; they were his friends. Gavin didn't want them subjected to someone else's leadership.

"Mmm," the doctor said, swabbing down the area with iodine. He stuck the syringe around the edge of the open wound.

Frowning, Gavin said, "Look, Doc, I don't want a three-week R & R back here because of this." He jabbed his finger down at the wound.

The doctor waited for the anesthetic to take hold and smiled at Gavin. "I know you don't want to get separated from your team, Captain, but this is bad enough to do it. If I release you back to your team and you go out on a mission and rip the stitches out, the wound will become reinfected."

"Not if you give me a steady supply of antibiotics to take," Gavin said. He could tell this doctor had just come over to the front. And he was probably a by-the-book kind, to boot.

Shaking his head, the doctor took the debridement sponge and squirted iodine into the wound cavity. "Sorry, Captain Jackson, I won't authorize that. Your wound is too deep. You're lucky it didn't go into your muscles. Take the three weeks of medical R & R and go to Kabul and chill out."

That was the last thing Gavin wanted. He felt no pain or discomfort from the debridement as the doctor meticulously scrubbed out every bit of the open wound. "Look, Doc," he pleaded, "I don't want my men going out there without me. They're safer under my leadership."

"Can't do it. Sorry." The nurse handed him the needle and thread and he began to close the wound one stitch at a time.

"How about you give my entire team a three-week R & R? Then we can go into Kabul together. They need a break."

Hartman's mouth curved slightly. "You're a pretty creative type, Captain Jackson."

"Look, my men need updated vaccinations. Couldn't you authorize my team off-line for that extra week because of that?" Gavin was giving the doctor the excuse he needed to authorize such a ploy. However, it was the veteran doctors who had spent a year in either Iraq or Afghanistan that understood what he was really asking for. Gavin had hope that if Hartman was a vet of the war, he'd do it.

"You know, Dr. Hartman," the nurse medic spoke up, "we are way behind on vaccination checkups for all the teams. I can accommodate their needs and rotate them through here." She smiled over at Jackson. "We've got forty-nine A teams in here. Maybe if you authorize Captain Jackson's team to stand down, I'll put them at the end of this roster. It would take a week to get around to vaccinating them. And as you know," she added, giving the young doctor a serious look, "we can't send these teams out there in summer without updated vaccinations."

Hartman nodded and considered the medic's request. "So, we're behind on vaccinations?"

Gavin couldn't believe his good luck. The woman was an officer like himself, a registered nurse, and had to be in her forties. He guessed she'd seen more than one tour at the front and was wise to the ways of getting things done for the troops when necessary. He gave her a nod of thanks, and she grinned back.

"Yes, sir, we are. Now, I could arrange this with your approval. The army isn't going to take notice of such things. One A team out of forty-nine that stands down for a week isn't a burp on the Pentagon's radar."

Hartman finished the knot, seeming pleased with his work. He put the needle and thread on the tray. Snapping off his latex gloves and tossing them on top, he told the nurse, "Do the footwork and I'll sign it."

Gavin watched the doctor quickly walk away to the next patient. "Thanks for catching on," he said to the nurse.

The woman set the tray on the gurney and began to place the dressing over the stitched wound. "Don't worry about it, Captain Jackson. He's green."

"Yeah," Gavin said grumpily, "I knew that."

She quickly bandaged his wound. "There. You're all set." She pulled off her gloves and dropped them on the tray. "I'm due for a break, so I'll go back to our office and get the orders created for you and your men."

Giving her a warm look, Gavin said, "You're a real angel." He read her name tag, G. Edwards. "Thank you, Lieutenant Edwards."

"My name is Gwen. And don't worry about it."

"Truthfully," Gavin told her in a quiet tone, "none of us really need any updated vaccinations."

Chuckling, Gwen took the tray and gave him a merry look. "Oh, I knew that, Captain Jackson, but Dr. Hartman doesn't. He arrived here two weeks ago and doesn't have a clue yet. I'll make sure your team is sent to Kabul for an extra week, and, of course, by the time I get around to your vaccination records, your wound should be plenty healed up. That way, we can release you and you can go back into action as a team."

"I owe you," Gavin said. "Thank you."

She winked. "Not to worry, Captain. You and your A teams are incredible and I'll do what I can within my duties to assist you when and where you need help. Enjoy Kabul for me."

Gavin felt like yelling triumphantly. Of course, he couldn't. As he watched Gwen move away and thread through the fifty or so gurneys and medical teams, he grinned. He slid off the gurney, realizing he must look funny with one pant leg gone and the other still on. He'd go back to his tent, tell his men what had transpired and change into a new set of trousers. After that, he'd go to the medical-unit headquarters to get his team's temporary orders for Kabul.

Walking out of the huge tent, Gavin saw the turbid gray clouds roiling overhead. In the summer, sudden thunderstorms could pop up and they were the only rain the desertlike area would receive. Some thunder rumbled far away and he walked carefully through the mud and puddles toward the row of tents where the A teams were housed.

As he did, he received some strange looks, but that was okay with him. His mind turned to Nike. How was she? Where was she? He'd been on the hill for two days acquainting the new A team with everything they needed to know. Gavin could have opted out of that role because of his wound, but he didn't. The medic on the other A team had kept him supplied with antibiotics, ensuring his wound would not become even more infected. Of course, Doc Hartman didn't know that and Gavin wasn't about to tell him, either. And certainly, no A team would push him off the hill, either. So many times, men who were cut, scratched or even suffering from flesh wounds like himself would not seek immediate medical treatment. They just didn't have the time or place to be picked up by a helicopter to get that sort of help.

Sloshing through the muddy ruts and divots made by men's boots, Gavin reached tent city. In no time, he told his team what was up, and there was a shout of triumph about going to Kabul for three weeks instead of the usual two. It was a well-earned rest for them, Gavin knew. Inside his tent, he got out of the destroyed pants and put on a new pair. As always, he'd remain in Afghan garb even in Kabul. Kabul wasn't safe for any American. And blending in with beards and Afghan clothes was a little insurance. Still, Kabul was considered barely stable and they would all carry weapons for protection. The Taliban was making a major push to take back the region.

Gavin headed off toward the BJS 60 squadron area. He knew where their HQ was and wanted to find Nike. He wondered if she was out on a flight or here at the base. Wherever she was, he had to know how she was. It didn't take him long to find the tent that housed the all-woman Apache team.

Each tent had a door. He opened the ops door and stepped inside. Removing his Afghan cap, he walked over to the red-haired woman at the desk.

"Excuse me, I'm looking for Captain Alexander."

The woman's huge gray eyes regarded him with a disconcerted look. He glanced down at the name tag on her green flight suit: E. Trayhern-Cantrell.

"Oh…and who are you?"

"I'm Captain Gavin Jackson. Nike and I know one another." He hooked a thumb over his shoulder. "I just arrived off a mission and I wanted to catch up with her. Can you tell me where she is?"

Grimacing, Emma looked around. Lucky for them everyone was over at the chow hall for breakfast. "Er, Captain," she began, her voice lowered, "there's been a problem."

Alarm swept through Gavin. "Is Nike all right?" He had visions of her being blown out of the air by a Taliban missile or her Apache burning and crashing.

Holding up her hand, Emma said, "No, no, nothing like that. Nike told me about you. So, I'm going to give you the straight scoop." She leaned forward and said, "Nike has been transferred out of here."

His brows shot up. "Why?"

"Captain, when we flew that mission to your hilltop and Nike gave up her seat so that Berkie could get the medical help he needed, we broke every rule in the book. We weren't supposed to do that, but we did."

"I don't understand. You saved his life by doing that," Gavin said, instantly flustered.

Emma stood and came around the desk. She didn't want anyone to hear this. "Captain, Nike and I took the fall for that decision. I lost my position as XO and she got transferred to the CH-47 squadron here at the camp."

Disbelief swept through him. "You mean…her CO got rid of her? She can't fly the Apache anymore?" Gavin was horrified.

"Captain, Nike came close to being court-martialed for what she did. Fortunately for both of us, the CO doesn't want to give the squadron a black eye by letting that happen. So, she sent Nike off to a transport squadron. She can fly an Apache once every seven days to keep up her skills, but that's all."

Gavin shook his head, reeling from the information. "But

she did nothing wrong. She saved a man's life, for God's sake!"

Emma held up her hand. "I agree with you, Captain, but there's nothing we can do about it. Nike could have been sent home to the U.S. or back to Greece. Her CO could have done a lot of things and didn't. This was the least slap on the hand that Nike could receive."

Stunned, Gavin stared at the tall, lean pilot. "I—I don't know what to say. I'm sorry this happened to the two of you. But my man's alive and on his way stateside now because of what you did. Doesn't your CO see that?"

"Our CO, Major Klein, is pretty savvy, Captain. She had no choice in this. If she'd let it go and the word got out on it, that would be bad for the squadron. She had to act."

"Dammit," Gavin whispered, shaking his head. He looked up at Emma. "I'm really sorry about this, Captain. I didn't think saving my man's life would screw up both your careers."

"Don't worry about it," Emma soothed, touching his slumped shoulder. "Neither of us is sorry we did it. And we didn't apologize for our actions in front of our CO, either. We are taking our lumps for this, but that's just part of being in the military."

Gavin knew it meant a hell of a lot more than that. Each woman's personnel jacket would have the reprimand in it. For the rest of their careers every time they tried to go to the next officer pay grade, that reprimand would be there. Rubbing his brow, he muttered, "This isn't right. Are you sure I can't do something to take those reprimands out of your jackets?"

Emma looked at him warmly. "Oh, how I wish you could, but you can't. One person cannot undo this type of reprimand. You're bucking one of the oldest rules in the

Apache book—neither pilot ever leaves the helicopter unless for safety reasons."

Gavin sighed. "I didn't mean to screw your career for you, Captain. Or Nike's. I know how much she loves flying the Apache and she's damn good at it."

"No disagreement there," Emma said. "What I'm hoping is that because it's summer and things heat up with the Taliban during this season our CO won't be able to do without her piloting skills. Right now, the CO can't find a replacement for her, which means one Apache is on the ground."

The ramifications were brutal and Gavin rubbed his beard. "So, she's officially with the transport squadron flying CH-47s? Permanently?"

"Yes, until further notice."

Gavin ached for Nike and wanted so badly to tell her he was sorry.

"You might go over to the transport HQ and find her there. She's still in our tent city but I don't know if she's home or out on a mission."

Grunting, Gavin put on his Afghan cap. "I'll do that, Captain. Thank you." He lifted his hand in farewell.

Of all things! Gavin tramped angrily through the mud and glared up at the clearing sky. In two days, Nike's whole career had been upended—by him. By his request. Even worse, he wondered if she'd be pissed off as hell at him and never want to see him again. Threading in and out between the tents, he finally found the BJS 60 group. In front of one tent was a young woman with blond hair.

"Excuse me, I'm looking for Nike Alexander's tent. Can you point it out?"

"Sure, right next to mine," she said, pointing to it.

"Thanks."

"She's not there."

Gavin looked at the name tag on the woman's flight suit: S. Gibson. "I'm Captain Gavin Jackson."

"Oh, yes, the A-team leader." She thrust out her slim hand. "I'm Sarah Gibson."

Gavin knew that his Afghan clothes might get him mistaken for a local instead of U.S. Army. No locals were allowed on the base for fear that the Taliban might get on the base in disguise. His skin was deeply suntanned and he could pass for an Afghan-born citizen. He didn't know how Sarah could tell his nationality except by how he spoke the English language.

"Sarah, do you know where Nike is?" His heart beat a little harder.

"No, I'm sorry, I don't," she said, shaking her head. "Since she got rotated out to the transport squadron, we rarely see one another. When I'm flying, she's here. When she's flying, I'm off duty."

Nodding, Gavin said, "Then I'll go to the transport HQ."

"If you don't learn anything, I can pass Nike a message for you. She always spoke of you in glowing terms."

Not now she isn't, Gavin thought grimly. "Could you tell her I'm back on base and doing fine? My team and I will be sent to Kabul for three weeks' R & R. Probably tomorrow morning. I'd really like to see her before I go." *And tell her just how damn sorry I am that I got her into this mess.* Even if Sarah gave her his message Nike might be so angry at him that she wouldn't care.

"Of course, Captain Jackson, I will." Sarah smiled brightly. "If you'll excuse me, I'm going on duty. Enjoy the R & R. I'm jealous."

Gavin tried to quell his fear as he walked into the HQ of

the transport squadron. It was a busy place with mostly male pilots coming and going, although he saw several female helicopter pilots. But Nike wasn't one of them. Standing near the door, Gavin searched the area to find out who might have the daily squadron flight roster. One man in back with red hair and freckles was at a huge chalkboard containing the name of every pilot and the flights for the day.

Aiming himself in that direction, Gavin quickly perused the names, twenty of them, on the huge green board. The very last name was *N. Alexander*. He smiled momentarily as he approached the enlisted man, a U.S. Army tech sergeant.

"I'm Captain Gavin Jackson," he began as an introduction.

"Yes, sir. What can I do for you?" the red-haired youth asked.

Reading the last name on his flight suit, Gavin said, "Sergeant Johnson, I need some info. You recently had Captain Nike Alexander rotated into your squadron. I'm trying to track her down. Can you help me?"

Johnson nodded. "Yes, sir." He turned and pointed to her name. "Right now, she's flying ammo and food to Alpha Hill in this valley." He read the chalked assignment on the board. "She left an hour ago. Should return, if all goes well, in about an hour from now."

Gavin realized Nike was resupplying the hill and the A team he'd just left that morning. How badly he'd wished he'd seen Nike.

"She'll be coming back in here once the mission is complete, sir."

Gavin nodded. "Thanks, Sergeant. After she's done with this flight, does she have the rest of the day off?"

Laughing, Johnson said, "Oh, no, sir. In fact—" he held up a sheaf of papers "—I was just going to the next chalkboard. Each one is a mission for each transport pilot. On good days, they might fly once or twice. On bad days, we're landing, loading up again and flying three to four times, depending upon the distance." He peered down at a paper. "She's slated to take an A team out to a place called Zor Barawul."

"Any other flights after that?"

Looking through the rest of the missions for the day, Johnson said, "No, sir, I don't see any. If all goes well, Captain Alexander should be done and out of here by chow time."

"Good. Thanks, Sergeant." Gavin turned on his heel and left the busy squadron headquarters.

Moving out into the muck and puddles left by earlier thunderstorms, Gavin sighed. He headed back to his own tent city to be with his team, but the whole time he thought about seeing Nike again. What would her reaction be? Anger or pleasure? Gavin couldn't guess and that drove him crazy. He liked to control his destiny and he couldn't control Nike's reaction to him.

The sky was showing blue among the white and gray shreds of cloud as the thunderstorms moved off to the east. Sun started to come out in slats here and there. The temperature rose and it looked like a good day ahead. Mind whirling, Gavin knew that flying transports was even more dangerous than flying an Apache. They were trundling workhorses, slow and unable to move quickly if targeted by the Taliban below. His heart ached with fear for her life. He'd just found her and now, dammit, through his own actions, he might have lost her.

All he could do was be at her tent when she returned.

Gavin couldn't quell the anxiety fluttering in his chest. He remembered starkly that one beautiful kiss they'd shared. He remembered Nike's fear of ever falling in love with a military man again. There were so many mountains to climb to reach her. In his gut, Gavin sensed Nike was worth every effort. But would she receive him warmly or with scorn? All he could do was stand at her tent and wait for his fate.

Chapter 12

"Hey, Jameela," Nike called to the woman as she approached the helicopter with her daughter. Nike had just arrived to pick up the current A team deployed to Zor Barawul. The mother was in her black burka, the crisscross oval showing only her eyes. Atefa was still on her crutches but Nike had learned that the medical facility at Bagram Air Base near Kabul was ready to fit her with a prosthetic leg.

Behind her, the load master, Sergeant Daryl Hanford, worked to unload all the medical and food supplies for the village. He got help from the new A team just arriving at the village.

"Hello," Jameela said, reaching out to grip Nike's extended, gloved hand.

Nike knew not to hug Jameela. That would have been against Moslem rules. Instead, she kissed each side of Jameela's hidden face, which was a standard greeting.

Jameela laughed and they pressed cheeks. Nike had been studying Pashto, and she knelt down and smiled into Atefa's bright and happy face. The little girl had a new set of crutches from America, far better than her old ones. "Hello, Atefa."

Shyly, Atefa smiled.

"Ready to go to Kabul?"

The little girl prattled on in Pashto. Nike had no idea what she was saying. Easing to her feet, she turned and looked at the progress at the CH-47. It had been unloaded, and Daryl waved to her to indicate everything was ready for takeoff. Since she didn't stay on the ground too long, Nike gestured for Jameela to bring her daughter forward.

They walked slowly, Jameela on one side of her daughter and Nike on the other. The storms of last night had made the once-flat spot a mire instead of a dust bowl. Half the village had gathered to watch them. Nike had been informed that Jameela would remain at Bagram, the air base outside the capital, for three weeks. Luckily for her, Nike would get to stay the night at the base.

Nike helped strap Jameela and her daughter into the nylon seat. By now, they understood it would be a roller-coaster ride until they could get away from the mountains and onto the brown desert plains. As Nike belted in and worked with her copilot, Lieutenant Barry Farnsworth from Portland, Oregon, she quickly went through the preflight checklist. Her heart lifted. She might have been kicked out of BJS 60, but at least she'd get a night at Bagram Air Base. That, she was looking forward to with relish.

At the O Club on Bagram Air Base outside of Kabul, Gavin nursed a cold beer and tried to get past his disappointment. Nike hadn't shown up at her tent. He'd gone looking for her but then one of his men had found him and told him they had fifteen minutes to get their gear together to catch a flight to Bagram for their R & R.

He looked around at the wooden tables filled with officers from all the military services. The long, U-shaped bar was made of plywood with plenty of bar stools. The room was crowded, with music, chatter and laughter. He should be happy, he thought, taking a swig of the ice-cold beer. The bubbles on his tongue from the beer always made him smile. There weren't many perks in this war, but getting a cold beer was one of them. It washed the mud of the war and their thirty-day missions out of his throat.

Gavin rested his back against the bar. For whatever reason, his gaze drifted to the main door of the O Club. It was nearly dark except for the lights around the entrance. For a moment, he thought he dreamed Nike Alexander entering in her olive-green flight uniform. It couldn't be! Heart pounding, Gavin slid off his stool, shock rolling through him. How did she get here? He didn't think. His instincts took the lead and he moved toward Nike.

Knots of men and women crowded around the many tables. It was tough to get around all of them. When Gavin managed to meet Nike, he saw her eyes go wide with shock.

"Gavin?" Nike blinked twice. Her pulse raced; she couldn't believe her eyes. Gone was his beard and his Afghan clothes. He was a suave urban American male in a pair of blue jeans and a short-sleeved white shirt. Even more, Gavin Jackson was drop-dead handsome. His jaw was square, his mouth sensual. The merriment in his blue eyes captured her. When his mouth curved, she felt heat shimmer from her breasts all the way down to her toes.

"You look different" was all she could say in her surprise over seeing him again.

"And you look beautiful," he said. Reaching out, he cupped her elbow. "Come on, I see an empty table in the corner. Let's grab it. I'll buy you a beer."

Head spinning, Nike followed and she soon found herself sitting at a small round table. It was fairly dark in this corner, with just enough light to see Gavin. Damn, but she couldn't stop looking at him. She'd never really seen his body because of his bulky Afghan clothes. Now he moved with the litheness of a cougar on the prowl. His arms were heavily muscled, his chest broad and powerful. Maybe it was his legs, those hard thighs, that made her throat go dry. She couldn't believe how dynamic and confident he appeared now. As Gavin turned, smiled at her with two beers in hand, Nike felt that she was in some kind of crazy, wonderful dream.

"Here you go," Gavin murmured. He set the beer in front of her, took a chair at her right elbow and sat down. Nike was wide-eyed and her curly black hair was wild, showing that she'd just recently flown. "Can you talk or are you still stunned?" He grinned.

Wrapping her hand around the chilled bottle of beer, Nike took a long swig. She closed her eyes and simply allowed the bubbles and the taste of the hops to wash down her dry throat. Once she set it down and found her voice, she gave him a silly grin. "I just can't believe you're here."

Gavin had the good grace to flush and gave her a bashful smile. "I never expected you to waltz through that door, either."

Nike took several more sips as his words registered. A waitress came over and she ordered a hamburger and French fries. So did Gavin. Nike rested her elbows on the table and stared at him. "How's your leg wound? I didn't know you were off Alpha Hill."

Feeling giddy, Gavin relayed the chain of events, during which he ordered another round. "Nike, I talked to Emma Trayhern-Cantrell and she told me what happened. I'm so sorry." How badly Gavin wanted to reach out and squeeze her arm, but he didn't dare. This was a military O Club and fraternization was not allowed. You could get drunk and fall on your face, but no kissing, holding hands or anything serious with the opposite sex. The exception was when the jukebox prompted couples to dance and the floor became crowded.

"Don't worry about it, Gavin. Emma and I knew we were breaking every rule in the book for Berkie."

His eyes were sad. "Then it's true? Your CO booted you out of BJS 60?"

"For the time being," Nike said, relishing the taste of her second beer.

"I didn't realize what this might do to your and Emma's careers," he muttered with sincere apology.

"I've lived long enough to know I'm not always going to do things right. Berkie was special to me. Well, all your guys were. When you said he was bleeding to death, all I could think about was his wife and baby daughter. I couldn't stand by and let him die."

"Well," Gavin said, his voice hoarse with emotion, "Berkie is on his way stateside. I don't know if you heard his update, but he's going to make it. Right now, he's on a C-5 Galaxy flight headed for Walter Reed hospital in Maryland. I know that Vickie, his wife, is flying in from Louisiana to meet him at the hospital after he gets through the entry process."

"Wonderful!" Nike said. "Is she bringing his daughter? I know he's only seen video of her on the computer."

"Yep," Gavin answered after taking a swig of his beer, "Francesca is going to be in her mother's arms when she's allowed to see Berkie. It's going to be one hell of a reunion."

Nike sighed with deep contentment. "Thanks for sharing all that with me, Gavin. It makes what we did worth it ten times over."

"Don't tell that to Major Klein. Next time, she'll crucify you."

"Oh, she's not like that usually," Nike said, smiling. "Dallas had to do it, Gavin. If she allowed us to get away with it, other pilots in other situations might think about abandoning their seat for another injured soldier. No, she was right and we were wrong. I'm willing to take the fall and so was Emma."

"You two are tough women warriors," Gavin said. His hand ached to hold hers.

"How long are you here for?" she asked. Gavin's face was deeply shadowed by the sparse light and it made him even more handsome—and so dangerous to her pounding heart. "And what happened to your beard?"

"I managed to wrangle three weeks here at Bagram for my team." He touched his chin. "I shaved it off today after we arrived. I'll have to let it grow back out. In three weeks, my mug will be covered again."

"You must have run screaming to the base barber." Nike chuckled. "Your hair is military-short, too." Indeed, his black hair shone with blue highlights beneath the light. There was a predatory quality to Gavin's face, especially with those large blue eyes. But it was his mouth that made her melt like hot butter. He couldn't know how much his looks influenced her wildly beating heart and no way would she ever admit it to him. Just sitting here at the table, their elbows almost touching, was like a fantasy.

Gavin grinned. "My team hit the barbershop posthaste," he agreed congenially. Touching his short hair, he said, "We just wanted to get cleaned up and feel like American men for a while."

"Over in the barracks where I'm staying, there's actually a tub, not just a shower in the room. I can hardly wait to get over there and take a long, luxurious hot bath. At our base it's outdoor stalls with piddling water coming out of the showerhead. This is real luxury."

"Bagram is beloved by all military branches," Gavin told her. "I know you're four months into your one-year tour here, but I'm sure you'll look for every chance to get a night or two at this base."

"That's one of the perks of being a transport pilot," Nike agreed. "In fact, tomorrow morning at 0700 I'm flying a supply of ordinance back to our camp."

Frowning, Gavin knew the CH-47 would be filled with ammunition of all types. "That's a dangerous run." If the Taliban got lucky and shot bullets—or worse, a missile—at the lumbering helicopter, it could be blown out of the sky. He'd seen it happen on four different occasions and nothing was ever found of the crews. Nothing. Heart contracting, he kept his mouth shut. The possibility of her dying in a situation like that nearly undid him. And yet, every day, every hour, they were in combat and bad things happened to good people.

Nike nodded and finished off her second beer. The waitress brought two oval plates filled with hamburgers and French fries. After putting dollops of ketchup and mustard on her hamburger, Nike ate it with complete enthusiasm.

For the next few minutes, there was silence because they were eating like there was no other pleasure in the world.

"Aren't we a couple of starved wolves?" she chortled. Between French fries she added, "Down in Peru, in our cave where BJS squadron lived, we had a pretty good chow hall. Our CO made sure that we got fresh fruits, veggies and eggs from Cusco. I always liked taking our transport helicopter into Cusco. My copilot and I would spend the night in that high-altitude city, do the tango, drink pisco and have a wonderful Peruvian meal. Then, we'd stagger back to our hotel and fall into bed. The next morning, we looked like hell, took hot showers and got into our civilian clothes to be driven back out to the airport." Chuckling fondly, Nike said, "We lived hard and died hard in Peru. We didn't lose that many women or Apaches, but our job was just as dangerous as it is here in Afghanistan."

"You traded jungle for desert. And instead of druggies, you got the Taliban."

"Bad guys exist all over this globe, unfortunately," Nike said. She finished off the French fries and gave him a silly grin. "I feel good. There's nothing like American food."

"But you're Greek."

"I know, but over the years of being in the States and then with the original BJS, I really got into American junk food." She patted her waist. "Good thing I come from a family of thin people. Otherwise, I'd be over the weight limit to fly the Apache." Nike chuckled.

"Do you really think you won't be allowed back into your Apache squadron?" he asked, getting serious. A shadow appeared in her eyes and she pursed her lips. It rankled his conscience that he had been the cause of her career demotion. Gavin knew the military very well. With that kind of reprimand in her personnel jacket, Nike could easily be overlooked for the next rank. Well, he had to live with the consequences of his actions whether he liked it or not.

"I don't think that Dallas will find another female pilot coming out of the Fort Rucker Apache training school," Nike said. "Not that many women wind up in the flight program and there's a lot of resistance to their being in the combat helicopter."

"Surely your squadron's exploits have shown them otherwise?"

"Over time the boys at the Pentagon stopped refuting our abilities." Nike grinned. "It's like pulling teeth, but we'll get more women into the Apache program. Like Maya, our CO down in Peru, said, we have to hold the energy and keep our intent clear. We know women can do the job as well as any man. Flying the Apache isn't about brawn. It's about brains and coordination."

A slow song came on the jukebox and Nike suddenly felt self-conscious.

"Come on. Dance with me. I like the idea of holding an Apache pilot with brains." Getting up, Gavin extended his hand so that Nike couldn't protest. He saw her eyes flare with several emotions, among them a desire to dance with him. He could feel it.

"Come on," he urged, gripping her hand. "You can do this. You're one of the bravest women I know, so don't say no."

Nike felt herself coming out of her chair. The dance floor was crowded as she followed Gavin out to the middle. When he turned and placed his hand on the small of her back and drew her closer, she came without resistance.

"See?" he whispered in a conspiratorial tone. "This isn't so bad, is it?" He led her expertly around on the floor.

Laughing a little, Nike said, "Did I have a horrified look on my face?"

Gavin drowned in her golden eyes. "Hey, you said you danced with the Latin boys down in Cusco, so why not here, too? How can I compete?"

"You don't have anything to worry about on that score," she said. He kept about six inches between them. Even though he could have used his hand to press her up against his body, he didn't. He gave her space that made her panic subside. Besides, Nike told herself, why not dance with Gavin? He was damn good at it.

"Oh? So I stack up pretty well?"

"Absolutely." He gave her a mirthful smile and she enjoyed the happiness in his blue eyes. Why not let go? She had in Cusco. She'd blown off the tension and danger and death that always surrounded them. Dancing with Gavin was a wonderful antidote to her flying in this country, too.

"I can tango, too," Gavin informed her, his grin increasing. "My mother loved ballroom dancing. I grew up knowing all of the different styles and steps. Competing as an amateur was her hobby."

"Well," Nike said, impressed, "you're good."

"You have no idea," he told her in a roughened tone, his lips near her ear.

Her flesh tingled wildly in the wake of his warm breath as it caressed the side of her face. For a moment, his hand squeezed hers a little more firmly. An ache rose in her body. She was so hungry for him that it wasn't even funny. Two years celibate had left her more than hungry, but she'd want Gavin in any condition. Something still made her hesitate. This wasn't love, right? This could just be a physical release. That's all she needed. At least, that's what she told herself.

"So," Gavin said quietly, "what's going on behind those beautiful eyes of yours? I see you want me."

"You are such a brazen dude."

He whirled her around and then brought her back into his arms. "I want this night with you, Nike. There don't have to be any strings, if that's what you want. One night together, that's it."

She looked deeply into his eyes and considered his request. "Just sex. And friendship."

Nike knew Gavin would be a good lover. She could tell by the way he monitored the strength of his hand around hers as they danced. She was wildly aware of his palm against the small of her back, and the way he sometimes caressed her with his thumb, as if stroking her. It reminded her she was a young woman with real needs. Maybe her grieving really was over and she hadn't realized it. Antonio would always be in her heart and her memory. Nike never wanted that to go away. When she loved, she loved deeply.

Finally, she couldn't stand it anymore. "Okay, let's get out of here. Your place or mine?"

"Mine," Gavin said confidently. He pulled her off the dance floor and smiled. "In the BOQ for the men, we each have a nice room to ourselves. I'll bet you have a roomie."

"Yes, I do. Does yours have a tub?"

"No, but we'll make do." Gavin smiled wickedly and led her out the door of the club.

Chapter 13

Just as they reached the male BOQ—Bachelor Officer's Quarters—an enemy mortar landed somewhere near the revetment area where all the helicopters were parked. Nike jumped and whirled around. Gavin automatically shielded her with his body.

Her eyes widened as mortars began to "walk" in their direction. Fire erupted when a helicopter was directly hit and flames roared into the air. Smoke belched into the dark sky, highlighted by the leaping flames. And then, when the aviation fuel on board the helicopter exploded, a huge reverberation of thunder was followed by a painful, ear-splitting boom.

Pressing her hands to her ears, Nike saw Gavin's tense, shadowed face as another explosion rocked a hangar nearby. "They're going to need us!" Nike yelled.

Nodding, Gavin gripped her upper arm. "Where's your flak jacket? You can't go anywhere without it."

He was right. All the festering desire that had bubbled up through Nike had vaporized in a split second. "I'm making a run for our barracks."

"Be careful! Meet me back here when this is over."

Nodding, Nike turned and hotfooted it down the line toward the women's BOQ that sat on the opposite side of the airport. People were running, grabbing their helmets, shrugging on their body armor and wrestling with their weapons. As Nike ran, the wind tearing at her, she saw that the Taliban's attack had been very successful. Three helicopters were on fire and utterly destroyed.

She ran around the end of the base and realized she had no weapon. Somewhere beyond the nine-foot-high fence, strung with razor-blade concertina wire over the top, were several Taliban mortar crews. Nike knew she could be a target with the flames leaping a hundred feet in the night sky behind her.

Changing course, she ran toward the burning wreckage and the fire crews now dousing the area with water. Better to take more time and go around the other end of the airstrip where it was safe in comparison.

Another round of mortars popped off. Nike could hear the hollow ring fired somewhere out in the night. To her shock, the mortars went toward the control tower, right where she was. With a strangled sound, Nike dove for the ground when she stopped hearing the whistle of a mortar screaming overhead. She hit the ground with a thud, the air knocked out of her. Rolling into a ball, her hands over her neck and head, she didn't have long to wait. The air-control tower was a two-story-tall brick building. The mortar landed on the side and about thirty feet from where Nike had burrowed into the ground. The next thing she knew, she felt a whoosh of hot air. In seconds, she was flying through the air, arms and legs akimbo.

When she struck earth once again, Nike yelled out in pain. She hit her shoulder and heard something pop. Barely conscious, she held her left arm tightly to her body, pain arcing up through her shoulder. Had she broken a collarbone? Worse, had she dislocated her shoulder? Groaning, Nike sat up, shaking her head. She spat out the mud and tried to reorient. People were running around like rats out of a drowning ship. Nothing seemed organized.

Holding her elbow tightly against her, Nike knew she had to get medical help. *Dammit, anyway!* Somehow she managed to get to her feet and fought to regain her balance.

The medical building was in high gear when Nike arrived. She saw men with torn pants or blown-off shirts. Some were burned, others dazed and bloody. Hesitating at the door, Nike knew she wasn't as seriously injured. Someone pushed her through the opened door.

"Get in there," a man ordered her in a gruff, no-nonsense tone.

Turning, Nike noted the white-haired doctor in a blood-spattered lab coat.

"Over there," he ordered her, pointing to an area where there were cubicles, each with a gurney.

Not hesitating, Nike headed to the dark-haired army medic with a stethoscope around her neck. Red-hot pain shot from her shoulder into her neck and the next thing Nike knew, she collapsed to her knees while still holding her left arm against her.

Gavin couldn't find Nike anywhere. Panic ate at him. In the grayness of dawn, he saw the black, smoking wreckage of three transport helicopters. He wondered if Nike's CH-47 was among the carnage. As he stood near the air-control tower that had missed several mortar rounds, he noticed how the ground around it was hollowed out in craters.

Where was Nike? He'd been over to the women's BOQ but hadn't found her. Nor was she waiting for him at his BOQ. Worriedly, he searched the red line of the dawn on the flat plain. Firefighting crews were putting out the final flames and smoldering fires around the helicopters. A number of other smaller buildings around the airstrip had been hit, as well. Rubbing his jaw, Gavin tried to search through the hundreds of crews working to reclaim what the Taliban just destroyed.

His heart ached with fear. Had Nike been hurt? Gavin turned on the heel of his boot and headed toward the medical area. Long ago he'd traded in his civilian clothes for a set of green fatigues, his combat boots, body armor and helmet. Normally, Bagram was never hit, but sometimes the Taliban took it upon themselves to get close enough to remind the Americans that no place in Afghanistan was safe from their strikes.

The air smelled of metal, smoke and burning wood. Panic started to curl up from his heart and he felt as though he was choking on fear. What if Nike was wounded? Dead? Blinking, Gavin refused to go there, though he knew that she'd tried to make it across the base to her barracks without any protective gear on. That made her vulnerable.

"Damn," he muttered, halting at the opened doors to the medical building. It looked like measured chaos inside. If the Taliban had struck to take out people, they'd succeeded. The wounded and bleeding sat everywhere on the floor, with medics and doctors working among them with quiet efficiency in triage mode. Peering inside the brightly lit area, Gavin scanned it for Nike. He did not spot her.

His gut told him to keep going, keep looking. He pushed through the entrance, winding his way through the medical teams and the nurses' station. He found an officer, an army nurse, and asked, "Have you admitted a Captain Nike Alexander?"

She looked up. "I don't have a clue, Captain. We haven't exactly had time to sit down and type all these people into our computer yet."

Nodding, Gavin said, "Mind if I look for her?"

"Go for it. Good luck."

After the nurse hurriedly left, Gavin turned and scanned the area. There were several curtained cubicles on the opposite side of the room. The people on the gurneys were all men. He searched every face in the entrance area and no Nike. Okay, if she wasn't here, maybe on the second floor, which was the surgical floor. Gavin picked his way to the stairs at the back of the room and quickly ascended them.

The surgical floor was also mayhem. Gurneys were filled with soldiers and airmen who had been wounded in the mortar attack. Blood dripped from one gurney, creating a large pool on the white tile floor. Medics hurried from one gurney to another checking stats, talking to the waiting patients lined up to go into the next available surgical theater.

None of them were Nike. Gavin couldn't still his anxiety. He knew in his heart he was falling in love with her. And now, she could be dead. *God, no, please don't let that happen,* he prayed as he made his way to the nurses' station.

"Excuse me," he called to a nurse who was updating records. "I'm looking for a woman, Captain Nike Alexander.

She may have been wounded in this attack. Can you tell me if she's here?"

The nurse gave him a harried look and stopped writing. She went to a large book on the desk and perused the list. "Sorry, Captain, no one here by that name," she said.

The only place left was the morgue. Gavin stared at her. "Are you sure?"

"Yes," she said firmly, "I'm sorry, she's not here."

Oh God. He stood and numbly watched the nurse return to her work. How could this be? One moment, Nike was walking with him to his BOQ. They were going to spend the night together. She'd been able to scale her fear of loss enough to be with him just once. But Gavin knew Nike wasn't like that. No matter what she said, he understood on a deeper level that she was reaching out to him. To love him. It was going to be a helluva lot more than sex. She cared about him, and he loved her.

He stood at the desk, his mind tumbling in shock and disbelief. He didn't want to go to the morgue. He didn't want to ask about her there. Tears burned in his eyes and Gavin blinked them back. His throat went tight with a forming lump. In that awful moment, Gavin realized that even though his bad relationship with Laurie had stung him, he was ready to try again. And Nike, in her own way, seemed to be working to trust once more, too. Why the hell did this attack have to come now? Gavin knew the answer: war was unpredictable. Death was a breath away. Nothing was stable and nothing could be counted on.

It has to be done. Mouth tasting of bitterness, Gavin worked his way out of the medical building. Last year, two of his men had been killed in a firefight and he'd had to identify them at the morgue here. He'd hated it then. He hated it now.

Dawn was pushing the night away, the red ribbon on the horizon turning pink and revealing a light blue sky in the wake of the cape of retreating night. The whole base felt tense and edgy. Grief ate away at Gavin. He remembered Nike's wish never to fall in love with a military man again for fear he would be ripped away from her. That her heart could not take a second shock like that. Well, now he was in her shoes. Making his way between large vehicles, the smell of diesel in the air, Gavin saw the morgue ahead. It was a single-story building painted the color of the desert. The doors were open. He saw several gurneys lined up with body bags on them. Was Nike in one of them?

Unable to look, he passed them and hurried inside to the desk. A young man of about eighteen looked up.

"Yes, sir?"

Swallowing hard, his voice barely a rasp, Gavin asked, "Do you have a female officer in here? Captain Nike Alexander?" He stood, not breathing, waiting, praying hard that he wouldn't hear the word *yes*.

The man scowled and looked through a sheaf of papers. "No, sir. No one by the name of Alexander, male or female."

Relief tunneled through Gavin. He felt faint for a moment. He'd been handed a reprieve. Releasing his held breath, he nodded. "Thanks," he muttered, and left.

Nike was just coming out of the BOQ when she spotted Gavin. He looked hard and upset, his eyes thundercloud-black. Worry was evident on his features. She gave him a wan smile and lifted her right hand.

"Gavin. Are you okay? I've been looking all over this base for you."

He saw her left arm in a sling. Halting, he said, "Are you all right? What happened?"

Grimacing, Nike told him the details. "As soon as they took X-rays, the doctor said I'd dislocated a ligament here on my shoulder out of what they call the AC joint. He got the ligament back in, thank God, but I've got orders to stand down for a lousy six weeks." She frowned at her left shoulder. "I can't lift my arm above my chest. That means no flying. I'm stuck behind a desk, dammit."

Closing his eyes for a moment, Gavin felt like a man who had just been given the greatest gift in the world. He opened them and clung to her golden gaze. "I—thought you were dead," he managed in a strangled whisper.

Nike stared at him. And then, it hit her hard and she managed a croak of despair. "I'm so sorry, Gavin." She reached out and gripped his arm. "There was no way to get hold of you."

"I know, I know," he said. Gripping her hand in his, eyes burning with withheld emotion, he rasped, "Nike, I understand your fear now. About losing someone you love to a bullet."

Shock bolted through her. Staring at Gavin, she realized he understood now as never before how she felt about Antonio being ripped out of her life. His hand was firm and warm. She'd been tense and nervous since the attack, but somehow, Gavin's protective presence just seemed to make her feel safe in an unsafe place. "It isn't pretty, is it?" she said in a low tone.

"No. It's not." He searched her eyes that held the shadows and memories of the past. "I looked everywhere for you. I—I eventually forced myself over to the morgue."

"Oh," Nike groaned. "I'm so sorry…."

And then, Nike knew that he really did love her. Gavin

might verbally spar with her but the look in his eyes told her the truth. Gulping, Nike shoved all that knowledge down deep inside her until she could deal with what it meant to her.

"It's not your fault. Things get crazy when a base is under attack."

She squeezed his hand. An ache built in her heart as she saw the devastation, the terror, in his gaze. "It's a hell of a way to understand my fear of a relationship with you. I'm sorry you had to find out this way."

"Nike, I don't want to live without you. I'm willing to risk everything to have some kind of a relationship with you on your terms."

His words melted through her pounding heart and touched her. Blinking through unexpected tears, Nike pulled her hand from his. Panic ate at her. This was serious. *He* was serious. There was no way she wanted to hurt him, but she had to. "I'm stuck in this war zone for another eight months, Gavin. What kind of a relationship could we have?"

"Catch as catch can?" he asked hopefully, the corners of his mouth pulling upward a tiny bit.

Hearing the hope, the pleading in his voice and seeing the stark need reflected in his blue eyes, Nike felt the last of her stubbornness dissolve. "I feel scared, so scared, Gavin." That was the truth. Nike felt terrorized by the realization he did love her. It wasn't just a game. It was real. Could she go there again?

"I understand your being scared." Reaching out, Gavin cupped her cheek. "Darling, we're just going to have to learn to be scared together. The last time this happened to you, you were alone. You had no one. Well, now you have me. I grant I'll be gone thirty days at a time in the field, but when we get back to base, we'll be together. I promise you that."

His eyes burned with such intensity that it seared the fright out of her. "All right," Nike quavered, "I believe you, Gavin."

Gavin stroked her cheek, knowing full well that fraternization was strictly prohibited. He could be in a lot of trouble. Worse, he could get Nike into more trouble than he already had. Quickly, he dropped his hand. Her cheeks burned a bright red. "We're going to make the most of this, Nike. We can't let fear tear us apart again. We'll live one day at a time. It's all anyone has."

Nodding, she slumped against the wooden building behind her. "You're right." She sighed. The feeling was there and she wanted so badly to say the words *I love you, too.* But she couldn't. Nike was still imprisoned by her loss as much as she felt this new love.

"I wish I was wrong," Gavin confided, coming close to her but keeping his hands to himself. "At least I get a reprieve from worrying about you. You're stuck back on base, which is a helluva lot safer than flying a helo."

"Don't remind me. I feel stifled in an office." And then more softly, "I won't stop thinking about you no matter what I'm doing."

Warmth spread across Gavin's chest. "Well," he said with a tender smile meant only for Nike, "it looks like we've made the best of a bad situation here. We might not have had the night we wanted, but we're alive and on the right page."

Despite the ache in her shoulder, Nike wanted to throw her one good arm around him, but that was impossible. "Six weeks…" Inwardly, she was relieved. Gavin was backing off. Maybe she needed that time at the desk to truly rethink her position with him and try to put the past to rest. To allow what she had with Gavin to blossom.

"What's the prognosis on your shoulder?"

"I'm on a mild painkiller for now," Nike whispered, her voice sounding off-key. "The doctor said it would take six weeks because I strained the ligament. They don't heal fast. He gave me a bunch of papers with exercises on them. At three weeks I'm to fly back here for another examination."

"At seven weeks I'll be back to base," Gavin said. "Maybe we could, you know, pick up where we left off before all hell broke loose?"

She grinned. Relief flooded her. Nike was sure she could figure this all out by then. "One way or another. I might not have the range of motion, but that's not going to stop me."

Gavin laughed softly. "Okay, sounds good. Where are you off to?"

"The doctor gave me orders to take the first transport back to our base. My helo was destroyed last night. My copilot will be coming back on the same flight. Once I get home, I need to go see my CO. I'm sure he'll put me on a desk and forget about me for six weeks."

"Wild horses don't do well in corrals," he teased her gently.

"Do you still get your three full weeks here?"

"Yes. They've asked all available personnel to help in the cleanup and I was going over to ops to get orders."

"Wouldn't it have been nice if the doc had told me to stay here at Bagram?"

Gavin rolled his eyes. "That would have been a miracle."

"Well," Nike told him, picking up her helmet bag in her

right hand, "I think we've seen plenty of miracles for one day, don't you?"

Gavin took her helmet bag and walked at her side as she headed for the airstrip. "You're right. A miracle did happen—between us."

"I'm still worried," Nike admitted. "I don't think I'll ever get over the fear of losing you, Gavin."

It hurt not to be able to reach out and touch her, hold her hand or place his arm around her just to give her a sense of protection. "You're not going to lose me. I promise. This is my second tour and I've got a year of experience under my belt. That will keep me alive."

How badly Nike wanted to believe that. The demons would resurface. Yet, the glimmer of love burning in his eyes fed her. Gave her hope. Could she really reach out and love him? Or would her fear drive him away?

Chapter 14

"When does Gavin get back to our base?" Emma asked as she sat with Nike in the chow hall. At noon it was packed, the noise high and the smell of cooked food permeating the area.

"Tonight if all goes well."

"Tonight?" Emma shook her head. "I suppose tomorrow he and his team will be flown out somewhere for thirty days?"

Slathering butter on a hot roll, Nike nodded. Her left arm hadn't seemed to make any progress over the last two weeks. She could lift it waist-high and then excruciating pain hit. Eating was an interesting proposition with only one and a half hands available to her. "Yes."

Emma ate her meat loaf after cutting it up into many dainty pieces. The perfectionist in her always expressed itself in many different ways. "That's not fair."

Snorting, Nike said, "When is war ever fair?"

"Or life, for that matter?" Emma rejoined, grinning.

"You got that right." Nike enjoyed the warm butter on the fragrant homemade roll. The late-August noontime was hot. A front was coming in and it was supposed to storm. Nike wasn't looking forward to that.

"Things seem to be falling apart over at BJS," Emma confided.

"Oh?" Nike raised her brows. "What's the scuttle-butt?"

Emma shrugged. "The bad news is that Becky Hammerschlag is the XO and she's terrible at it."

"You were a good one," Nike said.

"Everybody knows that. They keep coming to me, not Becky, with issues to resolve with Dallas."

"I'll bet Dallas isn't happy about that. Or Becky."

"No, not at all. I can't just ignore Becky and go around her to Dallas."

"Jumping chain-of-command is trouble for sure," Nike said. She spooned up some of her macaroni and cheese. "What else is going on?"

"Well—" Emma brightened "—some good news. In a way…"

"I can always use that. Tell me."

"It's good news for BJS but not for you. And it's good news for me, personally."

"Uh-oh," Nike murmured, "Dallas found another female pilot to replace me?" That meant that her secret hope to be pulled back into the BJS 60 squadron was squashed.

Emma nodded. "I'm sorry, Nike. I was holding out hope against hope that the pressures and demands on our services here would force Dallas to ask you to come back."

"Me, too," she said. "Oh, well."

"I'm sorry. We really miss you. You were our best pilot."

"Tell that to Dallas," she said, giving Emma a playful smile. Lifting her right hand, which had the last of the hot roll in it, Nike added, "Look, we knew we were breaking a cardinal rule when we picked up Berkie, but I'd do it all over again."

"I don't regret it, either. I'm just sorry that Dallas chose to focus on you instead of me."

"I'm the one who gave up the seat." She chuckled. "You stayed with the helicopter. Of course she's going to zero in on me."

"I don't think I'd take this as well as you are," Emma said glumly.

"Hey, you have a family military dynasty on your shoulders to carry," Nike chided with a grin. "Me? All I have is some disappointed parents and my big Greek extended family. But they understand and agree that I did the right thing. You? Well, if you'd gotten out of that seat, the media would have blitzed you over a transfer to a transport squadron." Shaking her head, Nike added, "No news about me being transferred as punishment because I'm not famous or in the media's eye like the Trayhern family is."

Emma sighed. "You're right. I've been catching all kinds of flak on the Internet blogs and even on CNN because of my demotion from XO."

"See?" Nike said, poking a finger in her direction. "I know the media is in love with the Trayherns. And what you did was heroic in my eyes. Maybe the media is chewing this up, but we saved a life, Emma. I'll answer for that decision with my God, not with anyone else. Especially not the media."

"Nike, you're one in a million. I'm proud to know you. I'm proud of what we did, punishment be damned. And I couldn't care less about the media sniping at me, but I know it impacts my whole family. That's what I don't like—them going after my mom, dad and sisters."

"Listen, they're Trayherns. They'll roll with it. A military family has the toughest of skins."

"Well, it hasn't done my career any good," Emma said.

"No, but I'm sure you'll distinguish yourself over here, and, in time, all will be forgiven. Me?" Nike grinned. "There's not much chance of me distinguishing myself as a transport pilot of men and ammo. So, as I see it, my days are numbered."

"Nike! You aren't going to leave the military are you?"

"I don't know. I'm up for reenlistment after this tour. Depending upon how it goes, I may get out. I didn't sign up to be a trash-hauler. I'm an Apache pilot and a damned good one. If the U.S. military can't use my services, then why stay in? I can find better work back in Greece where my talent can be used in the civilian sector."

"Let me talk to Dallas. You can't do this! We can't lose you, Nike! You're too good at what you do."

Nike held up her hand. "It's okay, Emma. I got myself into this pickle. I'll decide how I get myself out of it. Life doesn't end if I can't fly an Apache. I could land a nice, cushy job as a commercial helo pilot."

"Damn," Emma whispered, hanging her head. "You shouldn't even be thinking in those terms."

"We did it to ourselves," Nike reminded her, using the last of her roll to run through the gravy on her plate. "So tell me, you said there was good news for your family?"

"Oh, that…" She grimaced.

"Eat your food, Emma. You're so emotional. You can't let this impact you this way. I'm fine. I'm doing a good job over at the transport squadron."

"But you're not happy."

"I didn't say I was. Life isn't always fun, but we do our best."

"You were happy at BJS 60."

"Yes, I was. What I miss most of all is the camaraderie of the women."

Emma watched Nike eating her food. She seemed at peace despite everything. "The other good news is that my cousin, Rachel Trayhern, has just graduated from Apache flight school in Fort Rucker, Alabama. She's being assigned to BJS 60."

"Wow, you'll have a cousin here with you?" Nike was impressed. "Which family is she out of?"

"My uncle Noah's family. Rachel is one of four children. She's the oldest. My mother, Alyssa, was saying that even though her brother, Noah, was a Coast Guard officer for thirty years, all four of his children are in the military and flying. The flight gene is definitely from the Trayhern side of the family."

"Wow, that's great! Are you close with your cousins? I know in my family, we're tighter than fleas on a dog."

Emma laughed. "Yes, the whole family tries to get together. One year we'll go to Florida where Uncle Noah and Aunt Kit live and the next, we'll go to San Francisco, where my parents live. And then, they'll all try to make it to Philipsburg, Montana, where my uncle Morgan and aunt Laura live. It's a huge dim sum plate and it takes a lot of work to get everyone in one spot at one time."

"Mmm," Nike said, finishing off her applesauce. "I would think so if all the offspring are in the military."

"Rachel is a rock 'n' roll Apache pilot," Emma said, her voice reflecting pride in her cousin. "She's very competitive and aggressive."

"Just like an Apache pilot should be." Nike chuckled. She put her empty plate aside on the aluminum tray and picked up her white mug of coffee. "So, when is Rachel arriving?"

"A week from now."

"I didn't think the military would allow two family members in the same squadron."

"They don't allow brothers or sisters to serve together," Emma said. "They say nothing about cousins." With glee, she rubbed her hands together and gave Nike a huge grin.

"I'll bet your family is thrilled about this development. They must see you as the watchdog who can take care of Rachel while she learns the ropes."

Brightening, Emma began to eat once more. "They are thrilled. I'm excited to have her. We're good friends."

"When Rachel gets here, we must meet."

"Oh, that's a promise," Emma said enthusiastically.

"We can help her get situated with combat and Afghanistan. She could use our experience."

"For sure," Emma agreed. And then, her smile disappeared. "Have you been in touch with Gavin? Do you know when he's coming in from Kabul?"

"No way to get in touch with him. I checked at ops and his team is on a transport that will arrive here at 1700."

"Just in time for dinner."

"Maybe we can have one together," Nike said.

"You deserve a little happiness," Emma told her.

"Thanks," Nike whispered, meaning it. They sat for a

while in silence. The coolness in the huge tent area was wonderful compared to the heat and local storms. This place, in some ways, reminded her of home in Greece. The country blistered with dry summer heat and then chilled with icy temperatures in winter, but there was little snow unless one lived in the mountainous areas. Still, Nike looked forward to the moment when she could meet Gavin and his team. Her heart beat a little harder to underscore just how much she'd missed him in the last two weeks.

In the quiet moments at her desk, Nike would allow her heart to feel the love that had taken root within her. She knew he'd hurt her career but she'd forgiven him for that long ago. In the heat of battle, one didn't always think about such things. And in Nike's world view, a human life was a hell of a lot more important than a regulation. Since Bagram, she hadn't been able to stop thinking about Gavin. It seemed as if every few minutes, she'd replay some conversation they had. Or she'd recall that terrorized look in his eyes that told her the raw truth: he loved her. At first, Nike had felt it was a game with Gavin. Now, she knew it was not.

Gavin could hardly keep his face impassive. He watched Nike in her dark green flight suit, waiting as he and his men disembarked from the CH-47 helicopter. It was dusk; the skies were gray and churning. Soon, it would storm. She looked beautiful, her curly black hair about her face, a smile on her lips and those gold eyes shining with what he thought might be love—for him.

As he hefted off his duffel bag, he ordered his team to their already assigned tents. He told them he'd see them later. Turning, he walked with the huge bag across his left shoulder. Once more, he was in Afghan clothing.

"Hey," Gavin greeted her as he walked up to her. "Do you know how much I've missed you and our talks?" He kept his voice low so that others could not hear. It about killed him not to show affection. Her mouth was soft and parted, ripe for kissing.

"I'd like to hug you but I can't," she said with a grin, pointing to her arm.

"How's your left shoulder?" Gavin asked.

She held her hand out and could only move it waist-high. "I can't sleep on that side and I can't lift it beyond here. If I try to lean out and stretch it, I'm in pain. The doctor says the first three weeks are the worst."

Shaking his head, Gavin said, "That's no good. How's the desk job?"

"Boring as hell. How was Bagram?"

"Lonely without you." Gavin drilled a look into her widening eyes. "Is there anywhere we can go to be alone for a while?"

She grinned. "Yeah, my tent. Don't worry, the gals on either side of it won't say a peep about me having a male visitor." That was against regulations, too, but the female pilots protected one another. They would never go to the XO or CO about it. Sometimes, rules were meant to be broken.

"Good," Gavin said. "Lead the way." He hoisted his duffel up on his left shoulder once more.

In no time, they were at her tent. Nightfall was complete and they had flashlights to light their way through the tent city. Wind began to twirl around them as Nike opened up the tent flap to allow Gavin inside. She followed, turned and tied the flaps together. A small fan in the corner sitting on the ply-board floor gave some coolness against the high temperatures.

Gavin set his duffel near the entrance, turned and walked over to Nike. Although she did not wear her left arm in a sling any longer, he was aware of how painful it was to her. Gently, he laid his hand on her right shoulder. "Come here. I've been dreaming of kissing you for two weeks.…"

How wonderful it felt to come into his arms. Nike situated herself against him, her breasts beneath her flight suit pressing against his cotton Afghan clothes. His beard was growing once more and she felt the prickly hair against her cheek as their lips met. With a moan, Nike opened her lips and hungrily clung to his mouth. Their breathing changed, became ragged. He held her gently against him, his left arm around her right shoulder. His tongue moved slowly along her lower lip and a shudder of need rippled through Nike.

She wrapped her right arm around Gavin's broad shoulders. He smelled of the heat, and his arm felt strong and capable around her body. Her breasts ached to be touched and teased by him. Nike knew they couldn't dare make love here, even if her injured shoulder would allow it. Frustrated, she broke their hungry, wet kiss.

They stared at one another in the semidarkness. The only light came from a table lamp and it cast a weak beam around the interior of the warm tent. Gavin's eyes burned with need of her. After two years, Nike felt starved for a man's touch. Not just any man. Gavin.

"This is hell on earth," she muttered, reaching out and stroking his returning beard.

Her fingers trailed across his cheek and Gavin groaned inwardly. What would it be like to to have Nike touching his body? Nightly dreams had kept him tossing, turning and waking up over that very thing. He caught her hand and pressed it between his.

"Definitely," he agreed thickly. Gavin understood implicitly that Nike was in enough trouble. If he were found in here with her it would be another nail in the coffin of her career.

Nike moved away and went to sit on a canvas chair opposite the bed. "Sit down," she invited, gesturing to the cot.

Gavin did so—because if he didn't, he was going to kiss her again and again. His lower body ached with want of her. Nothing could be done about that right now. Sitting down, he opened his legs, rested his elbows on his thighs and clasped his hands. "I don't know what's worse—not seeing you at all or this."

Smiling, Nike sat back in the chair and cradled her left arm against her body. "I know. It's like going into a candy store and seeing all the goodies behind the glass. You can't reach them. They aren't yours."

Chuckling, Gavin said, "Exactly." He absorbed her quiet beauty. "How are you really?"

"I'm missing you. Our talks," Nike admitted quietly. They both spoke in low tones so no one could hear them outside the tent. It was the first time she'd ever admitted that to Gavin. She saw his eyes flare with surprise and then fill with warmth...and love. "My shoulder is progressing slowly. A lot more slowly than I want. The doctor keeps telling me at the four-week mark I'll have full range of motion back. If that happens, I'm going to be all over my CO to put me back on the ops missions and start flying again."

Gavin saw the frustration gleaming in her eyes. "There's no chance Dallas will take you back into BJS 60?"

Nike shook her head and shared Emma's information from lunch with him. "Hey, it's okay," she told him. "Berkie's alive. I'm okay with that, Gavin."

"I'm not," he growled, unhappy. "You should have been put up for a medal for your bravery, not removed from your squadron."

"I don't want to waste time talking about it, Gavin. I want our time to be about us." Her bold statement scared her but Nike tried to ignore the fear. This was real love. Not a game. And time wasn't on their side right now.

"You're right," he said.

"Where are they sending you?"

"They're dropping us off at the village of Kechelay. It's about two miles from the Pakistan border. We've got an outpost up in the mountains above that narrow valley where the village sits."

Nike tried to restrain her concern. "That's a hot spot right now, Gavin. We have pilots flying into that area and they're getting shot at. In fact, we had one CH-47 that had to remain on the ground at the village. They were off-loading food supplies for the village when the Taliban mortared it."

"What happened to the crew?"

"They were saved. No injuries. The Apache helo with them blew the Taliban mortar position up, but it was too late. We're out of pocket for a CH-47."

"I know Kechelay is a real dangerous area," he agreed, his voice grim. "We'll be taken to the outpost to relieve another A team that's spent its thirty days up there."

Fear gutted Nike. There was nothing safe about Gavin's job—ever. She remembered Alpha Hill, the memories fresh of Berkie, who had almost died there. His whole team would be put on the line once more. "What are you going to do up there? Be sitting ducks again like you were at Alpha Hill?"

Grinning, Gavin said, "Yes and no. We've got orders to rummage around at night and try to interdict the Taliban flowing through the valley. Kechelay is Afghan and the villagers are deathly afraid of Taliban retaliation on them and their people. Our job is to stop them from getting into that village. They've accepted U.S. food, clothing and medicine. We've got night scopes and goggles, so we'll be the hunter-killer team more than a bull's-eye for the Taliban." He saw the worry shadowing her eyes. The dim light caressed her beautiful face, emphasizing her cheeks and lips—lips that he wanted to capture and hear her moan with need of him. With a sigh, Gavin understood that wouldn't happen until he and his team returned to this base four weeks from now.

"It sounds pretty dangerous."

"It is," he said, not trying to sugarcoat it. "Flying a transport through these mountains and valleys is a crap shoot, too," he told her. "I'll worry about you."

"There's nothing to worry about," she said. "I'll probably be flying a desk until you return. The only thing I have to be concerned about is the Taliban attacking our base, and the odds of that are low."

"True," Gavin said. He smiled a little. "At least I won't have to stress about you."

Nike realized that would be a good thing. She wanted his focus on his duty because it would keep him alive—to come back to her. "I'll be safe here." Her voice lowered. "But I'll be worrying about you, Gavin." Again, the words *I love you* almost ripped out of her mouth. Nike felt she needed more time. And yet, the torture of not telling him that she was changing, that she was making a turn toward him and away from her past, ate her up inside.

Gavin rose to prepare for tomorrow morning's assignment. "Hey," he called, gently touching her cheek, "I have every reason to survive out there." Leaning down, he sought and found her lips. They were soft and yet firm. When her tongue met his, he groaned. This was a special hell. They could kiss but not make love.

Easing away from her mouth, Gavin whispered, "I love you, Nike. I think I did from the moment I laid eyes on you. I know we have a long way to go, and it takes our courage to get there." Straightening, he threaded his fingers through her soft, curly hair. She felt like warm silk. When she lifted her chin to meet and hold his gaze, Gavin said in an unsteady voice, "I'll come back in a month. We love one another. We've got something to build on. It's just going to take time."

As he opened the tent flap and then put his duffel on his shoulder, Nike stood up, her throat clogged with tears. And then Gavin disappeared into the night. Nike suddenly realized that she hadn't told him she loved him. *Why not?*

Closing the flaps and tying them, Nike had no answer except that she was still afraid. The fear of losing Gavin was ten times worse than before, simply because Nike realized she had fallen in love with this courageous soldier. She felt a helplessness similar to that she had felt in Peru. There was no way she could protect Gavin. The border area was rife with violent fights daily. For the second time, she had to wait and hope that the man she loved would return alive. It seemed unconscionable that she'd twice lose a man to war. But as they'd both said, war wasn't fair.

Chapter 15

Nike's pulse raced after she landed the CH-47 at Kechelay. Her copilot, Jeff Perkins, was a green lieutenant and this was his first flight after arriving in Afghanistan. She hooked her thumb across her shoulder.

"Jeff, help our load master with off-loading the cargo. Get it out of here ASAP. I don't want to stay on the ground any longer than we have to."

Jeff bobbed his blond head. "Yes, ma'am, pronto." He released his harness and squeezed between the seats.

Nike sat tensely in her seat, her helmet still on. She unharnessed, feeling uneasy. This was her first flight after being taken off medical waiver. After convincing her CO that her shoulder was healed enough at four weeks, Nike was back on line.

The village of Kechelay had a population of about one hundred. Several starving mangy dogs ran through the recently fallen mid-September snow. It was about three inches deep and the sky above threatened another round of snow showers. The cold air leaked into the helo as the ramp was lowered. Dividing her attention between the three villagers gathering about two hundred feet from the helicopter and her hardworking crew, Nike remained alert.

Somewhere across the valley were Gavin and his hunter-killer team. It was ironic that two days before he was due to be rotated back to the base, she was sent out to the very village where he and his men had been based. Missing him terribly, Nike wished for the hundredth time she'd told Gavin she loved him. Worse, every waking thought was of him. Their kisses in her tent… She wasn't sure what ached more: her heart or her body that wanted to love him and hold him—forever. Miserable, she looked out across the first snow upon the landscape, the tall mountains on the other side coated in white once more. Somewhere over there, Gavin and his men were probably hunkered down and sleeping in the daytime. His work was a nighttime affair and she didn't envy him. It was cold at eight thousand feet and she wondered how successful Gavin's team had been. Judging from the dark looks of those villagers, the fight with the Taliban was fierce in this area. Where were the rest of the villagers? Usually, when a supply copter came in, every able-bodied man was there to help off-load the boxes. Why only these three who had hatred in their faces here? Worse, the demand for Apaches at other firefights had left her without any protection on this mission.

Oh, how Nike wanted to see Gavin! Her arm was still sore and she realized she might have been released back to duty too early. Her pleading to the base doctor had convinced him to authorize her to go back and fly. Nike had passed all the tests he'd given, but she'd paid dearly for it later with aching pain. At least now, she could use her arm, and more than anything she wanted to throw it around Gavin's shoulders and kiss him breathless.

"Look out!"

The scream of warning came from Lieutenant Perkins. As Nike jerked around, she heard shots fired at close range. To her horror, the load master, Goldman, slammed to the ground, his head blown open. Jerking the .45 out of the holster, Nike leaped out of the seat and saw Lieutenant Perkins pulling out his .45 and backing up the helo's ramp.

Too late! Several Afghans, Taliban she realized too late, rushed the ramp, firing wildly. Bullets screamed into the CH-47, ricocheting around or exploding out of the thin metal skin.

Nike was lifting her .45 to aim at the leader, a man in a red turban with a black beard and equally black, angry-looking eyes, when she was struck. A bullet ricocheted off the inside of the helicopter and struck the side of her helmet, knocking her unconscious.

Pain throbbed through Nike's head. She groaned as she slowly regained consciousness. The first thing she realized was that her hands were tied together in front of her. Secondly, that it was cold and dark. Sitting up, she blinked through the pain. The left side of her face felt frozen. Reaching up with cold, trembling fingers, she felt dried blood all along her left cheekbone and jaw.

She looked around, gauging she'd been put into a small barn. The bleating of several sheep and goats confirmed this. And then, the memory of the attack on her men and her helicopter rushed back to Nike. She sat up, back against the wall of the rickety barn, remembering everything. Were both Jeff and Terry, the load master, dead? Nike knew the Taliban had initiated the attack. Those three men were not villagers, that was why she hadn't seen the able-bodied men from Kechelay there to help off-load the boxes. Why hadn't she picked up on that clue?

The door opened. Slats of light shot in and momentarily blinded her. Hearing the sheep bleat in terror, Nike squinted her eyes. Two of the Taliban appeared, armed and glaring down at her. "Get up!" one of them growled in stilted English.

Nike tried to get to her feet, but dizziness swept over her and she fell back onto the cold, hard ground. Hearing expletives in Pashto, Nike felt one of the men grab her by the right arm and yank her upward. She bit back a cry and wobbled unsteadily to her feet. But before she could regain her balance, her legs crumbled. There was nothing she could do about it. In the next second, blackness fell like a veil before her and she remembered nothing more.

Gavin was awakened by the GPS radio buzzing at his side, tearing him from badly needed sleep. He fumbled for the device in his pocket. He and his team were hiding in a cave near the valley floor. As he opened his eyes, he noticed it was snowing outside—again. More cold and poor visibility. To add to their troubles, the late-afternoon light was weak.

Gavin punched in a code and lifted the phone to his ear.

"Bluebird One. Over."

"Bluebird, this is Sand Hill Crane."

"Roger, Sand Hill Crane." Gavin rubbed his eyes. Why the hell was ops ringing him when they had at least two more hours of sleep before moving again? "What's going on?" he demanded, his voice thick with sleep.

"Bluebird, we have a situation at Kechelay. The CH-47 transport is overdue. We had a satellite over the area and the bird has been destroyed. We have a three-person crew missing. Over."

The fatigue vanished instantly. "We didn't hear anything, but we're across the valley and sleeping. Over."

"Roger that. You have orders to get over to Kechelay and try to locate our missing crew members. There are two men and one woman. Over."

"Names?" Gavin's heart raced. But then, he told himself it couldn't be Nike because she was still on medical leave.

"Captain Nike Alexander, Lieutenant Jeff Perkins and Sergeant Terry Goldman. Over."

Disbelief exploded through Gavin. "Are you sure?" His voice was urgent. Desperate. How in the hell had Nike managed to get off medical leave? The adrenaline rushed through his veins.

"Positive, Bluebird. We need you in there ASAP. Once you are in position, contact us. We have two Apaches and a CH-47 standing by if you need them. Over."

Son of a bitch! Gavin almost said it out loud. His other men were stirring now at the sound of his voice. Most of them were sitting up, yawning and throwing off the blankets. "Roger that, Sand Hill Crane. Out."

Gavin sat for a moment, GPS in hand, his mind tumbling with possibilities. The Taliban hated women in the military. Nike was in more trouble than the men. She would be tortured. Set up as an example in the village to stop women from even thinking about their independence. He pushed the GPS back into the pocket of his long brown wool coat and turned to his men. They had to move now. Every minute could mean the lives of Nike and her crew.

"Tell us everything!"

Nike tried to prepare herself for the coming blow. She sat in a chair, her arms bound behind her, her legs trussed. The side of her head exploded with bright light. Then the pain. Blood flowed out of her nose and into the corners of her mouth. It felt as if the man's hand had ripped off her head.

"Enough, Rasheed!"

Ears ringing, Nike spat out the blood flowing into her mouth and looked up. The left side of her face ached like fire. Rasheed, the one with the black beard, had been using his thick, opened hand to slap her into revealing military information. Two other Taliban remained nearby. Already, she could feel her left eye closing due to swelling. Thinking that her jaw had been broken, Nike breathed raggedly through her split lower lip. Fear ate through her pain. They'd dragged her out of the barn half-conscious. Her knees had taken the worst of it as one man on each side had grabbed her uniform by a shoulder and hauled her between them. Nike remembered, vaguely, many children and women behind burkas staring at them. Fear was etched on the children's faces—fear for her. Nike knew that when the Taliban entered a village receiving U.S. aid, they killed innocent people. Right now, Nike was sure villagers hid behind closed and locked doors. She didn't blame them. They had suffered brutality at the hands of the Taliban too many times.

For a moment, there was a hot argument between Black Beard and Brown Beard. Nike wished she knew more Pashto. Blinking, her eyesight blurred, she wondered if she'd sustained a concussion. Had the bullet to her helmet done more damage? Nike couldn't stand as the dizziness was severe.

It was warm in the room. At least she had that. Nike looked out the window and saw that darkness had fallen. White snowflakes, thick and big, twirled against the window. Fear engulfed her. She knew these men would kill her. Tears jammed into her eyes and she shut them, gulping heavily. She would never get to tell Gavin that she loved him. *Oh, God, please, let me live to tell him that. Just that...* In that moment, Nike felt the fear of the past dissolve. And with it, a bright burst of light through her heart—for Gavin. He'd loved her unerringly. He'd never wavered. He'd always been there for her, even though she'd been running away from him. The hot tears burned her cheeks and ran into her lips. The stinging pain intensified as they connected with her split lower lip. Unable to stop the tears, Nike surrendered to them—and to her love for Gavin. She would never see him again. That alone savaged her more than any beating at the hands of the Taliban. She would never be able to tell him she loved him. *Oh God, forgive me....*

Just as Rasheed reached forward to grab her by her hair once more, the door burst open.

Several men in white gear emerged, their rifles raised and firing. Rasheed had no time to reach for his weapon. He screamed and fell backward against the wall, blood gushing out of his throat. The other two men screamed as they were killed.

Gasping, Nike saw one of the invaders slam the door shut. The weapons all had silencers. The other three men surrounded her. The leader, heavily hidden in his white gear, pulled the hood away from his bearded face.

"Gavin!" she cried.

"Don't move," he ordered her hoarsely, handing his weapon to another team member. Unsheathing his knife, he quickly cut the ropes that bound her.

With a groan, Nike leaned forward. If not for Gavin catching her, she'd have nose-dived into the hard-packed dirt floor.

"Cap'n!" the man at the door whispered. "We gotta get outta here! I saw a light go on four doors down. There could be more Taliban staying here that we don't know about."

Gavin gripped her shoulders. "Nike, where're Goldman and Perkins?"

"Dead, I think," she rasped. Lifting her hand, she tried to wipe the blood flowing across her lips. "They died at the helo. We got attacked by Taliban while they were off-loading cargo."

Gavin grimly looked across his shoulder. "Chances are they burned the bodies when they blew up the helo."

There was terse agreement among the men. Nike tried not to cry.

"Okay, we're getting you out of here. Can you stand?"

"N-no." Nike touched her scalp where her helmet had been. She felt a deep wound in her scalp with blood still oozing. "I took a bullet to my helmet. I got knocked unconscious. I can't stand or I'll fall over."

"Okay, hang on," he urged her. In one smooth motion, he lifted Nike up and across his shoulders. He had her in a fireman's carry with the help of one of his men.

"Comfy?" he grunted to her. Nike hung like a big fur collar around his shoulders, her face near his. One of his team helped him put on his night goggles.

"I'm fine. Let's just get out of here."

Gavin nodded. They doused the lights and quickly stepped through the opened door.

Outside, Nike felt the soothing cold against her heated, throbbing face. Gavin moved quickly, as if she wasn't even around his shoulders. The team was silent. They swiftly moved outside the village, the light snow creating soundproofing as they went. In the dark, with night goggles on, they made their way toward the blackened remains of the helicopter.

Nike hung around Gavin's shoulders as his men quickly searched the smoldering wreckage of the CH-47. In no time, they found the half-burned bodies of the two men. Nike wanted to scream with grief. Her eyes burned as more tears began to fall. She heard Gavin curse softly.

"What now?" she asked thickly.

"We're meeting a CH-47 five clicks from here," he told her gruffly. "We'll put them in body bags and take them with us. How are you doing?"

"I'll live."

"Hang on...."

Gavin stood protectively by Nike as the doctor at the base examined her swollen face and blackened eyes. His team was brought in and a standby A team took over their mission. It took everything he had not to show his rage over her torture by the Taliban soldiers.

"Well," Dr. Greenwood said in a teasing tone to Nike, "This is going to get you two weeks' R & R at Bagram, Captain Alexander." He took gauze and continued to wipe away the dried blood from her jaw. "The X-rays came back. You got slapped around but good, though nothing is broken. That's the good news."

Nike grunted. She closed her eyes because each swipe of the gauze hurt like hell.

Gavin didn't care what the doctor thought so he reached out and held her hand. She sat on a gurney with her legs dangling over the side. Dr. Greenwood looked up but said nothing about their intimacy.

"What I'd recommend is pain pills for the next four days," the doctor said. "By then, the worst of the bruising and swelling will be over."

"Fine," Nike muttered impatiently. "All I want is a long, hot shower."

Chuckling, Dr. Greenwood nodded. "Just a few more minutes, Captain Alexander."

Gavin felt Nike squeeze his fingers in return. How badly he simply wanted to haul her into his arms, hold her and protect her. It wouldn't be long now.

"Your next stop before your shower is ops," the doctor told her, finishing up. "You have to give a preliminary report on your capture to your CO. You're not that injured that you can't do it."

"I understand," Nike said, touching her aching jaw. It wasn't broken, but several of her back teeth were loose. The doctor assured her they'd tighten up in a few days on their own.

"I'll escort you over there," Gavin told her as the doctor wrote a prescription.

"My office will issue you orders to Bagram for two weeks, Captain. Just drop by tomorrow anytime after 0900 to pick them up," the doctor said.

Gavin helped her off the gurney. She was still unsteady and clung to his arm.

"A wheelchair is in order," the doctor said, frowning. "The X-ray didn't show a problem, but you've got all the earmarks of a concussion, Captain. The dizziness should abate a lot by tomorrow morning. Get someone in your unit to check on you every couple of hours. If the dizziness doesn't lessen, come back and see me."

A medic brought over a wheelchair, and Nike gratefully sat down in it. Gavin leaned over and flipped over the foot panels so she could rest her boots. "If I'm still unable to walk straight tomorrow morning, you'll see me, Doc."

"Good night, Captain. Try to get some sleep," Dr. Greenwood said.

Gavin wheeled her out of the ward and into the lobby. He stopped and walked around and knelt down beside her. "Are you sure you feel like giving ops a report?" Searching her puffy, bruised face, he wanted to rage over what had been done to her.

"Positive. I want this behind me, Gavin. Tomorrow morning when I wake up, all I want to know I have to do is board a CH-47 and fly to Bagram."

Gavin gently touched some of her curly black hair near her temple. "I'll take you over to ops and hang out until you're done. Then—" and his voice lowered "—you're coming back to my tent and sleeping with me. I'm not leaving you alone tonight. Do you hear me?"

Nike gave him a blank look. "But I can't even kiss you…"

The wobble in her voice tore at him and tears gathered in her swollen eyes. "Babe, you don't have to do anything except let me hold you all night."

That sounded incredibly good to Nike. She sniffed, tried to wipe the tears off her swollen cheeks. She touched her lips and whispered in an off-key voice, "I want to kiss you.…"

"I'm a patient man. Right now, you need a safe place to unwind and let down. You went through a helluva lot."

Nodding, she managed, "I could have died."

Holding her fear-laden gaze, Gavin nodded. "But you didn't. You're here and you're alive."

"I'm a mess."

"Anyone would be after the beating you took," Gavin told her quietly. He slid his hand into hers. "Nike, you're in shock. Heavy shock. I know the symptoms when I see them. I'll be there for you. I promise."

Chapter 16

"This all seems like a nightmare," Nike told Gavin as they stood on the tarmac of Bagram Air Base. The September sky above was a combination of low-hanging gray, scudding clouds and bright blue sky peppered with slats of sunshine. However, it was sixty-three degrees Fahrenheit, and she was wrapped in her summer gear as they went toward ops.

Gavin walked close but kept his hands to himself. "It's over, Nike," he told her. "And you got some good out of it. Major Klein personally told you she was adding you back to the Apache roster. Your days of banishment are over." He saw her swollen face and lips lighten momentarily.

"Yeah, but I have to see a shrink here on base every friggin' day for fourteen days." Dallas had told her she had PTSD, post-traumatic stress disorder, due to her torture at the hands of the Taliban. She didn't deny it, but didn't want two weeks of rest at Bagram with Gavin at her side ruined like that.

"Small price to pay," he assured her. There was a lot of activity on the tarmac because it was early morning, and most flights went out then. Opening the door, they stepped inside the concrete building.

The air-conditioning was welcoming. The place was crowded with pilots, copilots and load masters at the L-shaped ops desk. Everyone was getting their flight plans and orders and making sure the materials that would be flown were really here and ready to be loaded. All Nike had to do was weave through the area to the personnel department where she and Gavin would hand over copies of their R & R orders.

Later, at Nike's BOQ barracks, Gavin stood with her in the lobby. Men were not allowed anywhere but this area in the two-story building. They sat down on a couch in the corner away from the main flow of traffic. "Do you have a plan?" she asked him.

Grinning, Gavin said, "Yeah, I do. I have a good Afghan friend who, oddly enough, is a Christian and Moslem. They're a rarity here, but they do exist. Captain Khalid Shaheen lives in Kabul. He was trained in America on Apaches and is the only Afghan to be flying one for us."

"I didn't know that," Nike said, impressed. "I thought I knew all the Apache pilots. I know there's a squadron based at Bagram."

"He's a part of that unit," Gavin told her. "I made friends with him during my first tour. We were in the south of the country at that time. More than once, Khalid saved our bacon out there against the Taliban. I went to thank him when my tour of duty was done. We became instant friends. He's one helluva guy."

"So, how does this have anything to do with us?"

"Khalid was American-educated. His father is a very

prominent and successful importer of Persian rugs. His mother is Irish. He and his family live in Kandahar." Gavin hooked his thumb over his shoulder. "His family has a summer home here in Kabul, as well, but the family stays in the south. Khalid uses the home here in Kabul as his own when they aren't here."

"Mmm," Nike said, "I'm beginning to get the picture. By any chance is your friend going to let us stay with him?"

With a grin, Gavin nodded. "Yes. Now, Khalid is not a promiscuous type. I've told him that we're serious about one another and he's offered two bedrooms to us."

"That's nice of him." Nike smiled wickedly.

"Very nice," Gavin said. "He's flying in the south right now, but he's left the key to his home with his housekeeper, who will cook and clean for us. She'll leave after the evening meal."

"That sounds like a slice of heaven," Nike murmured. "This is more than I ever expected," she said warmly.

"Khalid is a good guy. He stands with one foot in American culture and another in his country, living an interesting religious life in a Moslem world."

"He's got to be special."

"One of a kind," Gavin said. "Why don't you do what you have to do here and then we'll take a taxi into Kabul to his home."

Where had the first week gone? Nike finished taking a deliciously warm bath. Once more, she thanked the mysterious Khalid for his very modern home. Bathtubs were a rarity in Afghanistan. Those who could afford such plumbing had showers only. Most of the populace washed using a bucket or a bowl. Her stomach growled. It was 0800, the September sun barely peeking over the plain of Kabul, the sky a bright blue.

Patting herself dry with the thick yellow terry-cloth towel, Nike went to the mirror. It was partly steamed up, but she could see her face. Seven days had made an incredible change. The swelling was gone. The black under her eyes looked more like shadows and her split lip had finally healed. All her teeth were solid now and her jaw no longer hurt. Touching her cheek, she could still feel some tenderness, but she looked like her old self, more or less. Her hair was curled from the humidity and she ruffled through her black curls with her fingers to push it back into shape.

Sitting down on a stool, she pulled on white cotton socks, shimmied into a pair of jeans and donned a bright kelly-green tee. Khalid's home was cool and comfortable. Silently, she thanked the Apache pilot and wished that she could meet him in person to offer her appreciation for this gift he'd given her and Gavin.

Nike brushed her teeth and put on some makeup to hide the shadows beneath her eyes. After hanging up the yellow towel on a hook behind the door, Nike padded out into her spacious bedroom. If she didn't know she was in Afghanistan, the bedroom would have fooled her. Khalid, it turned out, had fallen in love with American quilts. They adorned every bed in the spacious three-thousand-square-foot home. And some smaller art fabric collages hung on the walls. Of course, his father's Persian rugs were everywhere across the bright red tile floors, too. Gavin had told her that Khalid would haunt the little towns in the U.S. to try and find another beautiful handmade quilt.

Opposite her queen-size bed hung a large quilt sporting rainbow colors and a wedding-ring design. Her room was painted pale orange and the quilt complemented the tone. She'd found out from Gavin that Khalid was not married. He would make some woman very, very happy someday. Not only did he come from a rich family, but he was Harvard-educated and had gone into the military. He worked now to get other Afghan pilots into the Apache program back at Fort Rucker. Khalid fiercely believed his countrymen should be educated so that they could handle any threats. He did not believe the U.S. and other countries should have to continue to shed their blood on the soil of his country. Afghans were independent and tried to pull themselves up by their own bootstraps. That was one of the many reasons Nike respected them.

Running a bristle brush through her hair, she gave herself one more look in the mirror. Today was the day. She and Gavin would make love. They slept together at night and he did exactly what he'd promised: he held her safe in his arms throughout the night. Never once had he made any overtures. He understood as few could that, being beat up as she had, she was in no shape for such things. She was grateful for his sensitivity, which only made her love him more. It had solidified her decision to love him fully, without her past as an anchor.

She found Gavin out in the large, airy kitchen. He was at the counter and had brought down two plates. She sat down on a leather stool at the counter. "Where's Rasa?" The thirty-year-old housekeeper had been with the Shaheen family since her birth. Rasa had never married and had been a faithful servant to Khalid at this house.

Gavin turned. "I gave her the day off." He saw Nike's eyes widen and then her luscious mouth curved faintly.

"I see. Great minds think alike."

"Do they?" He left the plates and sauntered over to the

breakfast counter. Leaning on the colorful hand-painted tiles, he held her sparkling golden gaze with his own.

Nike reached out and slid her fingers across his lower arm. Gavin looked incredibly masculine in his bright red T-shirt and jeans. "Oh, yes." His brows rose and a mischievous smile shadowed that wonderful mouth of his. "I don't know about you, but I'd like to schedule a brunch instead of a breakfast. Are you game?"

He picked up her hand and pressed a soft kiss into her palm. "More than game." And then he became serious. "Are you sure? Are you ready?"

"Definitely." She touched her healed lower lip. "Now, I can kiss you." Nike grinned playfully and squeezed his hand. "Let's go."

"Is this a dream?" he asked her.

"If it is, I want to take full part in it," Nike told him. As he approached her, she opened her arms to him. To her surprise, Gavin slid his arms beneath her thighs and back, lifting her off the chair and into his arms.

"Where are you taking me?" She laughed with delight.

"To *my* room," he said, grinning. Nike had placed her arm around his shoulders. Drowning in the desire burning in her eyes, Gavin took her down the hall, pushed open the door and brought her into his room.

Nike's eyes widened. Large, beautiful candles burned on the dark mahogany dresser and the nightstands on either side of the huge king-size bed. "Why, you—"

"I figured it was time," he told her gruffly as he deposited her gently on the bed.

Nike gazed up at him as he stood there, hands on his narrow hips and looking impossibly sexy. "We must have wonderful telepathy. How did you know?"

Touching his chest where his heart lay, he said teasingly, "I felt it here. Just like you did."

"Well, get over here...." Nike whispered, a catch in her voice. She pulled him down beside her on the gorgeous quilt that covered the bed. Its fall colors reminded her of autumn in New England. The bright yellow sunflowers around the border made her feel even more joyous.

Stretching out beside her, Gavin slid his arm beneath her neck as she rolled over onto her back. Heart pounding, he moved to her side. "Do you know how long I've wanted to kiss you?" he said. He leaned down, barely touching her smiling lips. Just feeling the lushness and curve of her beneath him was enough and he closed his eyes. He brushed his mouth lightly against hers.

Nike sighed as his tongue gently moved across her lower lip. She felt as if she were being caressed by a butterfly. Gavin understood this first time was going to be tender and gentle. As the kiss deepened slightly, Nike surrendered completely. She never wanted to go back. It was too good, this feeling of intimacy and deep passion. His warm breath became as ragged as hers. Wrapping her arms around his shoulders, she moaned as his lean, hard body connected fully with hers. The moment was magical as Nike drowned in his mouth and then felt his hand sliding softly against her cheek.

In the back of her whirling mind, Nike realized that as hard as Gavin could be, he had the incredible sensitivity and gentleness to woo her with light touches here and there, a stroke across her cheek, a teasing sip of his mouth against hers. With him, she felt safe. He was healing to her brutalized spirit.

Gavin slid his hand beneath her tee, his fingers lingering slowly along her rib cage. He caressed her flesh and moved under her shirt to the fullness of her breast. He inhaled her gasp of pleasure as he found the hard nipple. Easing the tee up and off her, Gavin allowed it to drop to the floor. For a moment, he had to look into her face, into those eyes. He got lost in their golden depths and how they shone with a hungry need of him. His desire now turning feverish, he leaned down and placed his lips upon the nub. As he suckled her, she moaned and her hips ground into his.

Nike's world exploded into a powerful heat that leaped to life between her legs. Each suckling movement drove her deeper and deeper into starving need of Gavin. Gasping, she pulled off his T-shirt and watched the powerful muscles in his chest and arms. His chest was covered with dark hair, which only added to his sexiness. Giving him a wicked smile, she whispered, "It's my turn." She forced him onto his back and quickly unsnapped his jeans. In a few moments, she'd pulled them and his boxers off him, along with his shoes. As he lay naked, she appreciated Gavin as never before, and she ran her hand admiringly across his hard thigh. She whispered, "You are beautiful, like a Greek god."

Laughing, Gavin sat up and quickly removed her jeans, shoes and socks. "And you're a goddess," he rasped, pinning her on her back, his hands splaying out across her arms. "And you're mine," he growled, pressing his hips into hers. Nike's eyes shuttered closed as he allowed her to see just how much he wanted her.

"I can't wait," she whispered unsteadily. And she gripped his arms and forced him onto his back. Without waiting, she mounted him.

"I like this," Gavin said, bringing his hands around her hips. He lifted her and gently brought her down upon his hardened length. Her fingers dug convulsively into his shoulders as he arched and slid within her hot, wet body. Groaning, he held himself in check since he didn't want to hurt her. She'd been hurt enough lately, and he wasn't about to be a part of that.

"Easy," he said, holding her hips above his. "Take your time...."

Her world disintegrating, all Nike could feel was a huge pressure entering her. It didn't hurt, but at the same time, she was hungry to inhale Gavin into her. The years without sex made her feel as if she couldn't accommodate Gavin. When he leaned upward, his lips capturing a nipple, she automatically surged forward, engulfing and absorbing him fully into herself. The electrical jolts, the pleasure from her nipples down to the juncture between her thighs, had eased the transit. Now, his hands were firmly and slowly moving her back and forth. A moan rose in her throat and all Nike could do was breathe, a complete slave to this man who played her body like a fine instrument.

The world shuttered closed on Nike as Gavin's hands, his lips and the hard movement of his hips grinding into hers conspired against her. She wanted to please him as much as he was pleasing her, but that wasn't happening. All she could do was feel the heat, the liquid, the building explosion occurring within herself. Her body contracted violently. She cried out, rigid, her fingers digging deeply into his chest. And then, her world became a volcano erupting and all she could do was cry out in relief, the pleasure so intense that it just kept rippling again and again like a tsunami rolling wildly and unchecked within her. All that time as she spun out into the brilliant white light, the sensation of no body surrounding her anymore, Gavin kept up the rhythm to give her maximum pleasure.

How long it lasted, Nike had no idea. She felt herself

crumpling against him, felt his arms like bands around her, holding her tightly, forever. The smell of sweat, the sensation of it trickling down her temple, her body still convulsing with joy over the incredible release and him groaning beneath her, was all she could fathom. She had no thinking mind left. The only sensations were relief, pleasure, love and wanting Gavin over and over again. Peripherally, Nike knew he had climaxed and she pressed her face against the juncture of his jaw and shoulder, utterly spent. A loose smile of contentment pulled at her lips. Her hand moved weakly across his dark-haired chest and followed the curve of his neck until she cupped his recently shaven face. She lay against him, breathing hard with him. Just the way he trailed his fingers down her back to her hips told her how much he truly loved her.

"Wow…" Nike whispered. It took all her strength to lift her head enough to look into his face. She thrilled to the thundercloud look in his blue eyes. They burned with passion—for her. "Wow…"

He chuckled, his hand coming across her hips and caressing her. "Wow is right." Just absorbing Nike's gleaming gold eyes told Gavin everything he wanted to know. They lay together, connected, and he never wanted to let her go. Flattening his hand against the small of her back, he slowly raised his hips. He saw the pleasure come to her eyes and to her parting lips. "Give me a few minutes and I'll be ready to wow you all over again."

Grinning, Nike leaned down and moved her lips softly against his smiling mouth. She could feel Gavin monitoring the amount of strength he applied to her. She was fragile in many ways and he sensed that and loved her at that level. Her lower body burned with memory and she loved how he remained inside her. Nothing had ever seemed so right to her. "I'm already ready." Nike laughed breathily.

"It's been two years," Gavin told her, reaching up and framing her smiling face. "You stored up a lot of loving in that time."

Moving her hips teasingly, she could already feel him filling her once more. That was amazing in itself. "I did." She reveled in his hands framing her face. "Maybe we should skip brunch and go to a late lunch."

That moment of her husky laughter, the heat of her body, the look in her eyes conspired within Gavin. "Maybe supper."

"I'm hungry for *you*," she whispered, becoming more serious. "I've wanted you since I first laid eyes on you. I fought it for a long time, but that's the truth." Nike's brows dipped as his hands came to rest on her hips. "I love you. I should have told you that back at base before all that stuff happened. You have no idea how many times I regretted not telling you when I was tied up in that barn in that village. That hurt me the most—not having had the courage to tell you how I really felt."

Whispering her name, Gavin trailed his fingers across her cheek. He saw the tears in her eyes and his heart contracted with pain. "Listen, you did the best you could, darling. Learning to let yourself love again is tough. I understood that." And then he gave her a boyish smile, hoping to lighten the guilt she carried. "I loved you from the moment I saw you. And I knew I'd eventually get you. All I needed to do was show you that you didn't need to be afraid to love me."

Nodding, Nike lay down across him, her head coming to rest next to his jaw. "I'm glad you didn't give up, Gavin. I wanted you, I really did. But I was so scared." She felt him move his hands down across her drying back. It was a touch of the butterfly once more, as if absorbing and taking her pain away from her.

"We're all scared, Nike," he told her, his voice rough with emotion. "And we each had to take the time to surmount those fears. In the end, we're pretty courageous people. We love one another. And yes, we have this tour to get through, but we'll do it. It will be good because we'll get to know one another over that time. Together." He eased her chin up with his hand so that their eyes met. "Together. You hear me?"

Nodding, Nike leaned over and caressed his lips. "Together." She saw a satisfied look come to Gavin's face.

"Marry me."

Shocked and laughing, Nike pushed herself up into a sitting position upon him once more. "You have this all figured out, don't you?"

Gavin eyed her innocently. "Hey, I have a lot of time to think while I'm out there in the boonies for thirty days at a time." Gavin reached up and caressed her curly hair. "I figure that your parents will probably want us to marry over in Greece."

"Got that right," Nike said, laughing. "My parents would have a kitten if you wanted us to marry in the States."

Gavin smoothed his hands down the length of her back and across her hips. "You can e-mail them anytime you want. Luckily for us, Khalid has satellite here at the house."

"Maybe later," she whispered, lying back down upon him and nestling her brow next to his jaw. "Right now, all I want to do is be with you, Gavin. I want to make this next week last forever."

He pressed a kiss to her brow. "Listen, forever is going to last a lot longer than this week. I'm looking forward to a long, long life with you."

Closing her eyes, Nike whispered, "That's all I want, too, Gavin. I love you so much."

Harlequin offers a romance for every mood!
See below for a sneak peek
from our paranormal romance line,
Silhouette® Nocturne™.
Enjoy a preview of REUNION by USA TODAY
bestselling author Lindsay McKenna.

Aella closed her eyes and sensed a distinct shift, like movement from the world around her to the unseen world.

She opened her eyes. And had a slight shock at the man standing ten feet away. He wasn't just any man. Her heart leaped and pounded. He reminded her of a fierce warrior from an ancient civilization. Incan? She wasn't sure but she felt his deep power and masculinity.

I'm Aella. Are you the guardian of this sacred site? she asked, hoping her telepathy was strong.

Fox's entire body soared with joy. Fox struggled to put his personal pleasure aside.

Greetings, Aella. I'm the assistant guardian to this sacred area. You may call me Fox. How can I be of service to you, Aella? he asked.

I'm searching for a green sphere. A legend says that the Emperor Pachacuti had seven emerald spheres created for the Emerald Key necklace. He had seven of his priestesses and priests travel the world to hide these spheres from evil forces. It is said that when all seven spheres are found, restrung and worn, that Light will return to the Earth. The fourth sphere is here, at your sacred site. Are you aware of it? Aella held her breath. She loved looking at him, especially his sensual mouth. The desire to kiss him came out of nowhere.

Fox was stunned by the request. *I know of the Emerald Key necklace because I served the emperor at the time it was created. However, I did not realize that one of the spheres is here.*

Aella felt sad. Why? Every time she looked at Fox, her heart felt as if it would tear out of her chest. *May I stay in touch with you as I work with this site?* she asked.

Of course. Fox wanted nothing more than to be here with her. To absorb her ephemeral beauty and hear her speak once more.

Aella's spirit lifted. What *was* this strange connection between them? Her curiosity was strong, but she had more pressing matters. In the next few days, Aella knew her life would change forever. How, she had no idea....

Look for REUNION
by USA TODAY bestselling author
Lindsay McKenna,
available April 2010,
only from Silhouette® Nocturne™.

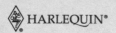

HARLEQUIN®

INTRIGUE

WILL THIS REUNITED FAMILY
BE STRONG ENOUGH TO EXPOSE
A LURKING KILLER?

FIND OUT IN THIS ALL-NEW
THRILLING TRILOGY FROM TOP
HARLEQUIN INTRIGUE AUTHOR

B.J. DANIELS

WHITEHORSE
MONTANA

Winchester Ranch

GUN-SHY BRIDE—*April 2010*

HITCHED—*May 2010*

TWELVE-GAUGE GUARDIAN—
June 2010

HARLEQUIN® *Romance*®

ROMANCE, RIVALRY
AND A FAMILY REUNITED

THE BRIDES *of* BELLA ROSA

William Valentine and his beloved wife, Lucia, live
a beautiful life together, but when his former love Rosa
and the secret family they had together resurface,
an instant rivalry is formed. Can these families
get through the past and come together as one?

―――――

Step into the world of Bella Rosa
beginning this April with

Beauty and the Reclusive Prince
by

RAYE MORGAN

Eight volumes to collect and treasure!

www.eHarlequin.com

HRI7650

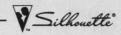

SPECIAL EDITION

**INTRODUCING A BRAND-NEW MINISERIES
FROM *USA TODAY* BESTSELLING AUTHOR**

KASEY MICHAELS

SECOND-CHANCE BRIDAL

At twenty-eight, widowed single mother
Elizabeth Carstairs thinks she's left love behind
forever....until she meets Will Hollingsbrook.
Her sons' new baseball coach is the handsomest
man she's ever seen—and the more time they
spend together, the more undeniable the
connection between them. But can Elizabeth
leave the past behind and open her heart to
a second chance at love?

FIND OUT IN

SUDDENLY A BRIDE

*Available in April
wherever books are sold.*

Visit Silhouette Books at www.eHarlequin.com

SSE65517

REQUEST YOUR FREE BOOKS!

2 FREE NOVELS PLUS 2 FREE GIFTS!

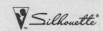

Sparked by Danger, Fueled by Passion.